20 68

WHEN DEMOCRACY FAILS,
HOW FAR WOULD YOU GO TO GET IT BACK?

20

68

Emma Adair

This is the second published edition
First published in 2020 by Adair Gallery
Copyright © Adair Gallery 2022
The moral right of the author has been asserted

10 9 8 7 6 5 4 3 2

ISBN (Paperback) 978-0-6489399-2-4
ISBN (eBook) 978-0-6489399-6-2

A catalogue record for this
book is available from the
National Library of Australia

Typesetting by Typography Studio

For Melbourne

1

April stood breathless pressed against the laneway wall. She was listening for anyone who had seen her climb the gate. She'd heard stories of the lanes so often she'd thought she remembered exploring them when she was little. Now she was sure she hadn't. The walls collapsing in above her and the uneven stones underfoot were inconstant with her imagination. As a group walked toward the lane, past, then away she waited, unflinching, for silence, determined for the ninth night to find the entrance to the Lamasery.

Each night, April had evaluated a different lane. The first eight lanes were distinctly different from each other. Some were narrow and deep, she presumed ideal to hide a door. Others were wide with smooth flat walls, unlikely to have successfully concealed decades of secret movements. Her preliminary assessment had identified two lanes which seemed possible. After surveying the final three, a more forensic plan would need to be devised.

April found tonight's lane, however, deceptive—while wide initially, it became thinner and had begun to curve. Methodically scaling and interrogating loose panels, locked doors and vacant shopfronts, April abruptly realised she could no longer see the gate. Apprehension nudged her resolve. Just as she was about to retreat, she heard a mechanical buzzing somewhere beyond the bend. Abandoning her technique, she followed the noise and discovered a splice between two buildings. The hum was married to light spilling out from a basement illuminating the adjoining path. Disbanding hesitation she crept toward the light.

Arriving at a shield of boxes and bins, April could faintly hear laughter. Carefully separating two stacks of crates, she could see clearly through an exposed window into the basement. Behind the glass were rows of heads facing a serious young man pacing in front of a whiteboard alternating writing, contemplating and talking. April sat and watched. His audience broke into laughter again and he transformed revealing a cheeky grin which made him look even younger; she thought he might be close to her age. The room applauded and he bowed. Mesmerised, angry shouting in the distance jolted her from the trance. In a panic she jumped up and twisted to run back to the lane, clipping the crates in her haste. One by one they fell crashing onto the ground tumbling over each other in a cascade of metal and wood, an explosion of chimes filled the chasm.

Paralysed, April waited. If she could hear them clapping, they would certainly have heard her clumsy mistake. Blood rushed in her ears. Searching for a solution, unable to focus on anything other than the crates now blocking her only exit, she resorted to praying for the walls to swallow her.

He appeared in the opening with rage in his eyes and a weapon in his hand which he quickly withdrew when he registered she – bathed in warm light from the basement – was trembling. He put his hands in the air to show he was not a threat then beckoned her to come to him. April ceased shaking. He did not appear to want to hurt her. As the adrenaline drained away she stepped forward, cautiously navigating the obstructions, untrusting of her quivering ankles. He moved out of the alcove, signalled she was free to leave and held his finger to his lips instructing her to remain silent. As she moved forward, he moved back giving her space to walk away. She slipped back into the lane and he whispered, "What are you doing here? It's not safe here."

A good question. They must not receive visitors often because he looked as shocked as she felt. April considered the safest response. She didn't know whether this was the Lamasery. She didn't know whether this man was a sympathiser or why he was in the lane or what instruction he had been giving. April looked into his eyes staring at her in disbelief and realised if she wanted answers she would need to admit the real reason she was in the lane. He didn't seem dangerous. On the contrary, he seemed concerned for her which was odd but she supposed it was because she was both visibly terrified and unarmed. She chose trust.

"I was trying to find Lidia."

He paled. He tensed. But did not reach for his weapon. He continued to stare as if working through the same consideration she had given him. He too chose trust.

"I know Lidia. Why do you want to find her?"

In that moment in the dark lane in the middle of the night in the grasp of a stranger and devoid of any rational instinct to not destroy her career or put her family at risk, April had no answer. Why was she here? Because of an old story. Because she wanted to understand the past. Because she wanted the truth.

"I am trying to find the Lamasery." She froze.

He seemed content with the explanation and pondered the situation.

"I will ask Lidia if she wants to meet you. You know about the Lamasery.... She will want to know how. Meet me tomorrow night halfway down St Kilda Pier at ten."

She nodded and he disappeared into the darkness. She whispered at his back, "What's your name?"

He called under his breath, "Diamond."

2

On her fourteenth birthday, trying frantically to entertain a house full of unruly teenagers, April's father regaled the tale of the Lamasery. In his spookiest tone, he warned, while they had been told decades had passed since the last sympathisers had been active in the City, Lidia was actually alive and continued to lead them from the Lamasery. Constructed over two centuries ago, the Lamasery could only be discovered if you had been shown its exact location. Consequently, the Department had never been able to find Lidia and legend foretold Lidia was planning their return and would rise again at the fifty year anniversary. April's friends sniggered, impervious to his theatrics, but something in his telling made April suspect there was more truth than fiction. Afterward, she had tried to extract details about the Lamasery and Lidia from her father but, known for his discipline, once recomposed, it was futile. She was reminded that this was a story, not history, and her fixation on revolutionaries and their mysterious hideouts was dismissed. Determined to secure a mathematics cadetship at the Department, April relented and focused on school. Eventually, she forgot about the Lamasery.

Two weeks prior however, while transfixed on solving an equation at work, gossip wafted into her office on the breeze from two chatterboxes sitting on the bench outside her window. One commented they had noticed an increased security presence at the Department and the other replied it was because Lidia had been sighted several times in the past month, but neither knew where or why. Walking away, each exclaimed they had thought Lidia was dead. The memory of her party came flooding back.

Revisiting the myth with the benefit of hindsight and her completed education, the prospect that the legend was true was not as implausible as her father had ardently insisted. In the beginning, the Department was meant to be just like any other government only without elections. The Department Assembly had been formed when the government and shadow government – after signing the bipartisan Formation Agreement on election eve – appointed themselves to govern, as one, unopposed for twenty years. At the time, Anna, Lidia's wife, and her supporters tried to appeal the legitimacy of the Department Assembly's self-appointment to the Court of Justice but failed; after which Anna was sentenced to twenty-six years in prison for inciting civil unrest and being a danger to public safety.

After Anna was incarcerated, Lidia was said to have had continued to coordinate the sympathisers and, over time, had become their leader. As expiry of the Formation Agreement neared, the sympathisers had feared the Department Assembly was planning on overstaying its term and tried to overthrow it on the eighteen year anniversary of formation. In an effort to retain order, Police had defensively killed over two thousand sympathisers as they infiltrated Department facilities all over the City. An investigation concluded that the Anniversary Attacks as they became known had been planned for years. As punishment, a further five thousand sympathisers were sentenced to death. No one had expected the Department Assembly to respond so vengefully.

With blame assigned triumphantly, grasping renewed validity, the Department Assembly revised the Formation Agreement, removing its expiry permanently. Grieving sympathisers were too shocked to put up a fight; everyone else weary and desperate for normalcy.

On the day of Anna's release, eight years after the Anniversary Attacks, the Department Assembly executed Anna, without a trial, on the steps of the Court of Justice claiming an intention to incite anarchy. Anna's execution provoked a riot of ten thousand sympathisers who, still raw, stormed and then burnt down the Court. In response, the Department Assembly closed the CBD to anyone without a permit, constructed security check points at every street corner and the lanes were gated. As a result, cracks in the Department Assembly's defence of its own existence were permanently cast, ever-expanding, threatening to fragment ever since.

The story of Anna and Lidia was intimately intertwined with the history of the City but April had never heard anyone speculate Lidia might actually be alive, let alone in connection with the Department. Lidia hadn't been seen since the night of Anna's execution and was presumed dead. They were taught in school that, with no leaders, the sympathisers eventually gave up. She, too, had noticed more security but dismissed the observation as coincidence. In light of their past determination, upon reflection, April didn't find the possibility that sympathisers were still among them at all improbable. Sceptical that presenting this evidence to her father would yield a confession, she decided to break into his filing cabinet.

3

April's father worked for the Department as a senior meteor-ologist. He had little choice as some years after completing his qualification, the Department had become the sole employer for any industry requiring analysis of data. While he never con-fessed as much, April believed he may have been a sympathiser in his youth, though the best evidence she could offer was the subtle pride in his voice when he recalled the day his workplace had been infiltrated during the Anniversary Attacks. But there was also the locked filing cabinet, which he maintained was full of comic books he didn't want grubbied by sticky fingers but April suspected contained government records from the days before the Department.

During their weekly Wednesday dinner, April took leave during dessert and snuck into the hallway, retrieving her father's keys from the left pocket of his overcoat. Then, with a shameful lack of guilt and an equally shameful amount of skill, silently rummaged through each drawer. She was embarrassed to find they were lined with mint comics, mummified in plastic. Interesting she had never once seen her father read one. Peering between the editions and conscious of the conspicuous amount of time she had been away from the table she found a hidden folder tucked at the back of the last drawer. There was an emblem glued on the front, it looked like a shield entwined with a clock and a bird. Underneath the shield were three words. April plucked a selection of pages, mindful that taking the whole folder would be too brazen should her father view its contents regularly, and restored the scene of her crime.

After dinner, April walked back to her apartment, for the first time wary of the security cameras which had long since dissolved into the background; her heightened sensitivity aroused by the guilt. Once safely in the privacy of her bedroom she inspected the pages. Some were copies in her father's handwriting, others originals in a second softer and less rigid style. Blushing, April realised immediately that these were love letters to someone who signed their letters only with anonymous declarations of love. Affection was reciprocated in the replies which April knew to be her father's through his distinctive abrasive cursive; not a loving style by any measure. The other person's letters described living within the Lamasery. The contents were vague and details non-specific; the letters, not dated, did not divulge when this love transpired. A collection of statements of longing and frustration carefully crafted suspended in time, drenched in context only relevant to the other. April, wracked with guilt, stopped reading, tempted to run back and return them but this would have to wait until dinner next week. Without envelopes, it was unclear how these letters were being transferred between her father and the Lamasery, but their exist-ence indicated someone must know its location.

She knew from her father's story the Lamasery existed and now – as confirmed in these letters – she knew the Lamasery was in the lanes. There were many, but the lanes which were over two centuries old were confined to the north-west of the CBD. With the fifty year anniversary of formation looming, an air of vigilance had descended and the Department Assembly was frequently amplifying deterrents. April wasn't sure what the punishment for trespassing was these days, but there were only a handful of lanes where the Lamasery could have been built and remained secret all this time.

4

Lidia was nestled in the corner of the window seat with her back against the architrave. Glancing at the clock, she could hear someone climbing the stairs. The impossibly strict routines put in place, scheduling access to and from the Lamasery, had kept them concealed thus far. Unplanned footsteps more often than not carried news of death. In the beginning, she feared these impromptu visits but, as the years passed, so did her capacity to maintain constant concern their location would be discovered. This visitor was compounding a disastrous month. Anna had been extremely famous and by association Lidia's face, even with the natural camouflage of time, was highly recognisable. She'd required several dental procedures which forced her to visit a specialised surgery and in a confluence of bad timing she had been recognised by three people in a week. In her experience, one sighting amounted to nothing but two created validation after which rumours flowed hotly; she would need to remain confined until calm returned.

Fortunately there were few tasks which could not be undertaken by others or within the Lamasery. In decades past there had been successive years where Lidia had not needed to leave the sanctuary and occasions important enough to compel her presence had withered. The last had been the death of her mother. A cherished six weeks at her bedside enough to vent and settle all outstanding grievances in preparedness for a final goodbye; her sweetest time since Anna's death. Routine medical treatment and diagnoses were typically conducted at the Lamasery by physicians she trusted but there had been several minor surgeries which had required her to leave. There had also been one serious cut and she had been taken urgently to a hospital where she was able to be kept hidden. All plans and counterplans which had been meticulously devised and practiced. Thankfully, as she otherwise would not have survived.

The ancient door handle turned. Even after holding her wife while she bled to death in her arms, on bleak days Lidia allowed herself to indulge on the rush of excitement that Anna might be home at last. A fantasy as delicious as it was agonising evaporated as Diamond appeared in the doorway. She was relieved it was someone she knew. He smiled and she relaxed; he was not carrying a death notice. Diamond had been delivering for the Lamasery since he was a boy and had managed to retain an aptitude for evading attention. He was waiting to be invited to sit – aware, if Lidia was so inclined, that he could be in for a tirade about protocols – however she was distracted and he decided get to the point before she had the chance.

"I was briefing last night and found a girl in the lane spying on us. She was looking for you. She knew about the Lamasery,"

He paused but she continued to stare into the distance. "I said I would tell you she was looking for you."

Her position remained unchanged but irritation now etched around her eyes. She turned to look at him still standing in the doorway. "What is this girl's name?"

He hadn't asked. Awkwardly he shrugged, trying to feign that his oversight had been forced.

"I assume if you don't know her name you also don't know who she is or why she wants to find me?" He nodded, careful not to hang his head or look sullen.

"Find out who she is and how she knows about the Lamasery. Everyone who knows I'm here has an emergency channel. There is no reason for this girl to be searching for me."

Lidia pointed at the door, graciously dismissing him without tackling how careless he had been for a matter so unworthy of the risk; he promptly raced back down the stairs. Over the years, conjecture often found its way back to her ears, largely exaggerated and sometimes outright lies, but never about the Lamasery. Unmoved on her familiar window sill she felt concerned. What strange girl is trying to find her in the lanes? Even if the girl had heard of the Lamasery it must have originated from someone close; its actual location in the lanes was entrusted to so few. But who would expose her location, necessitating a reckless hunt? Speculating was useless. Diamond would come back with answers. Lidia turned her mind back to watching for the signal which, if all was in order, would arrive today. Lucky for Diamond her attention was needed elsewhere.

5

Scraping and scratching echoed in the dining hall as the churn of feeding workers rotated around April as she ate. When she first started at the Department, lunch was her favourite novelty. Department staff were provided one main meal and were encouraged to eat with their colleagues. April had been delighted. She didn't need to worry about fuel which gave her more time to focus on her work; with the added bonus of less food to carry home from the market. Her father, annoyed as she had gushed, retorted with an eye roll. April, confused by his aversion, had pressed him until he blurted it was absurd everyone had to eat the same food together like prisoners. She hadn't considered the implied oppression of a convenient and free meal she didn't have to prepare and was confounded by his apparently justified outrage. This bone of contention a rare glimpse into her father's true temperament. Looking down at her meal now, and the adjacent row of identical meals, she felt uneasy.

Her conviction something was amiss had driven April to the lane. She had initially felt satisfied her instincts had been validated but now, upon reflection, questioned the origin of her own suspicions. She had been fixated on what was kept from her but now, on the cusp of discovery, she wondered why. Her quest was for truth, but she was not discontented. She was happy with her life, but nonetheless couldn't reconcile what she was told with what she felt.

Her food was cold and she threw what was left in the bin and headed to that fateful bench below her office window to consider whether to go to the Pier. She ran her fingers over the detailing in the metal frame. This bench. Had it not existed in this place she would still be blissfully unaware of these lofty secrets threatening the relationship she'd once blindly believed in but now doubted. How many benches could claim to have wrought such turmoil? She suspected all battles were planned sitting down before being fought upright.

Diamond had suggested St Kilda Pier. Seemed dramatic. Surely there were more comfortable places to meet. She was thankful she had scant information and so little time to prevent her from overthinking the ludicrous situation. She knew she would go. She was not afraid of Diamond and her curiosity was insatiable, to walk away from a mystery begging solving was unfathomable. She was less concerned for her safety than for the information she may wish she had not discovered. Was her life a lie because she was not aware of these people, or would her life be the same tomorrow regardless of Diamond's revelations?

Walking back into the building down the hallway, past doors to other offices, she considered whether she should tell her father where she was going. She had realised any kind of dialogue would invariably include the expectation of her divulging her source. She could lie. She had no knowledge of whether these people were known to her father, or he known to them, or whether they were friends or enemies. Absolute honesty was not sensible.

April's office was lined with charts and boards. The room was more than she, at her low status, would normally be entitled however the previous occupant had retired the week prior to her commencing in the building and, fortunately for her, this distinguished location was the only space available. The person who retired had left without feeling any desire to vacate the space. As a result, the walls were covered with discarded briefs and musings. The cosy feel conjured by the remains of someone else's career invited April into her office as though it were home and she dared not disturb the layered montage, fearful she would alter the affect. She suspected also the established décor made her seem more knowledgeable. Visitors would often enter and spend their meeting examining her face, then the walls, trying to reconcile her youth with the apparent vast experience.

Today, the familiar cocoon of unfinished science and math was a welcome break from the disorientation of the mandated lunch she couldn't bring herself to swallow. The afternoon waned under the strain of the impending rendezvous with Diamond. She attended a seminar to distract herself from what remained of the day until it was time to leave familiarity and confront her requital.

6

Patrice stared down the boardroom table with a resolve that struck fear into the attendants hearts' deterring anyone who dared to speak against her, which they never did and rarely had cause. Razor-sharp, her determination – the source of her intimidatory manner – was also the feature which made her unbeatable. It was less that she worked harder than others, rather that her focus was so intense. Her mastery of everything she encountered was inevitable. She was as impressive in person as she was by reputation.

Her rise at the Department had been vicious yet she was unscathed. Her signature move to identify an irrefutable saving in the presence of two superiors – one of whom would benefit and one who would not – made her difficult to contest and thus her assent continued unabated. Her calculatedness was so famous that, like today, her meetings were full of witnesses, utterly unrequired, vying for a first-hand anecdote.

Unfortunately for her admirers, there was nothing particularly controversial on the agenda; there were also few rungs remaining on the ladder. She was ostensibly where she had aimed to be and, having reached the apex, every day was more invigorating than the last. She was both exhausted and elated.

Department life suited Patrice instantly. She had chosen the perfect partner in her first year – her counterpart in every way – and he had delivered. Their relationship cemented her place, and his, in the pool of leadership talent and as they conquered each test together, every victory made her more certain of her ideas and merit. Their impact on the Department evoked such adoration their wedding had been celebrated like a union of the City's darlings. After which, as a married woman, Patrice sought to shed her reservedness and become ruthless in her work. A feat she had witnessed over the years, only achievable in the rebirth of marriage. She had once felt the pressure for children. Patrice had been looking forward to motherhood until she started in this new role and, engrossed, shelved the compulsion. Her husband, ever aligned, also wanted to settle in a suitable portfolio before inviting the inevitable drain of children on their time. The years of work leading to this appointment had be worth every sacrifice and she had the fortitude to keep pace now finally the one directing design.

Patrice went back to her office at Department East to check in with her support team before heading to the Dome. Part of her responsibilities as a new Department Manager included oversight of City Services, mundane in name yet one of the most exciting portfolios. Her proven ability to make precise decisions under pressure had won her the opportunity over the other claimants, including her husband. Patrice's first weeks in the role were heavenly. The glazed Dome atop the building contained lush greenery and carefully placed reflective technology which enabled the facility to remain concealed as a private garden. Designed to give a complete view of the City, the command centre monitored and mimicked perfectly the Department's most sensitive operations; its existence unknown to anyone outside the Department Assembly. To learn of the Dome and its function, described by her predecessor upon their departure, was transcending—only to be outshone when Patrice was introduced to the facility. Her esteemed colleague had failed to mention the marvel of technological excellence was speckled with roses, conifers and lavender.

Another thrill was her position at the centre of the floor, with access to every service, camera and microphone in the City. There had been several incidents during her handover, however Patrice was only required to take control in the event of a shutdown of Department Central. The Dome's permeant staff, under the watchful command of the Chief Operator, were well-equipped to continue with their daily monitoring, recording and surveillance without her interference. Her role was to absorb and learn in the hope she'd never need to call on the knowledge.

There were no urgent items at the office and, swiftly changing out of her suit into nondescript streetwear, Patrice was content to disappear for the rest of the day. It was exceedingly problematic finding time to get to the Dome without rousing suspicions in her office; none of her staff had clearance sufficient for her to be able to tell them where she was going. Perhaps this was a good time to get pregnant after all, she thought; alibis were hard to fake when in a position so rigorously demanding. She must ask her forbears for some advice in this regard, while blessed with an abundance of talents lying wasn't one of them. A task for another day. This time, she had announced to a chorus of romantics sighing in unison, that it was her anniversary dinner and she must away to get prepared for an evening of unbridled extravagance. Not technically a lie, just an overestimation by several hours as to the start of her date. Nevertheless, once satisfied the bait was taken she left.

Access through the lanes into a web of walkways and hallways and underpasses ensured the entrance to the Dome was thoroughly complicated and thereby extremely secure. It had taken weeks to learn the path by thought exercise. According to one of the maintenance technicians, the route had never been written and had only every been learned by repetition. Unwilling to flout tradition, Patrice had committed the way to memory and now navigated the path seamlessly. Today she needed to master the transport console. She had been focusing on critical infrastructure and emergency responses and, satisfied with her understanding, now wanted to absorb the protocol for the Dome to take control of the railways.

7

The Pier had been fitted to enable covert surveillance from the Lamasery so Lidia could monitor recruitment or appoint new security or conduct vetting where strangers were involved. Diamond remembered his first time on the other side of this setup before being invited to the Lamasery—not that he understood the significance at the time. Lidia was watching and, sensing potential for a new recruit, had briefed him on the information she required. Originally when this protocol was designed, the Lamasery would be able to talk directly to their representative. However, hesitation was often met with lethal suspicion and the practice had proved to be fatal more than once. As a result, the distraction of their virtual presence was abandoned.

April stepped onto the Pier and began walking. She could see Diamond in the distance perched against the frame of a shelter. She supposed she should have been scared, or at least a little nervous, but at this hour she was just tired. She was normally in bed. As she drew closer he came into focus and was rather striking. On the night they met, she had been watching him through the basement window for some time, however backlit by moonlight his silhouette was intriguing. April had quite often been told she was effortlessly beautiful, something she suspected meant: it is clear you have put in no effort and fortunately your face is well-proportioned. Diamond however was effortless. Despite the attraction, she was determined to persist with the elaborate backstory she'd concocted during the marathon between the end of work and this inconveniently located liaison. A few metres from him now, she could see he was smiling at her thoughtfully. He sprang away from the timber and took her hand in both of his.

"Hello, I'm relieved you decided to meet me. I thought you might change your mind?"

"I'm looking for answers. You said you knew Lidia?"

"Let's sit on the dividing wall so we can look at the City skyline." He nodded and pointed down the boardwalk.

She almost laughed. Of all the eventualities she had cautiously considered, being tricked into a date was not one of them. It occurred to her this savant may not even know Lidia and she had been fooled by her ambition. They sat facing the spectacular view.

"Thanks for coming. Before you say anything, let me go first."

She raised an eyebrow and waited.

"I'm sure you came here tonight intending on not telling me who you really are." Spot on, she thought. "However I want to explain the situation we are in."

Unconvinced, April interjected. "Who is we?"

Diamond held up his hand.

"I'm representing Lidia. As I was saying, you are looking for answers but it is extremely unusual that you came to be able to ask the questions. It is clear to Lidia you must have no comprehension of the context in which you are asking these questions, in order to be able to ask them at all."

April was mystified by the riddle but thought she knew what he was trying to say.

"Do you suspect I know something I'm not supposed to know?"

He raised his hands to the sky.

"Yes! But what I meant is, if you don't tell me who you really are and who told you where to find Lidia, we will never be able to answer your questions."

He was right. She had not appreciated the rarity of the fragments she had been able to piece together; her only option was to be honest or walk away. Lies would not produce answers. Unexpectedly, the breathtaking nightscape helped her think.

"I can see you need some time. I'm not in a hurry, I have bought some water. Would you like a bottle?" She was distracted from the predicament; what a ridiculous question to be asking at such a loaded moment.

"I would like some water, thank you." Apparently dalliance was Diamond's style when trying to coax information out of startled women in the dead of night. She deflected. "You are clearly a part of this world I have stumbled upon. I do want answers but I don't want to reveal how I came to obtain this information. There is someone else involved. If you were in my situation, what would you do?"

He looked taken aback by her seeking his counsel but obliged.

"If the person who told you about the Lamasery has this information because they obtained it from Lidia, it's likely they are, or were, associates at some point. Alternatively, they are an adversary. Without you telling me who told you, there is no way to know. It is, as I said, unusual for you to have this information in conjunction with having no idea as to the type of relationship between this mystery person and Lidia."

A good summary of her quandary but not helpful in deciding a way forward. Bottle in hand, she turned to look into his piercing eyes. "Diamond, this person is not a person whose confidence I would betray under any circumstances. Even in circumstances such as this. I'm sorry, I need to go."

He deflated. "I understand. Perhaps I can arrange for you to meet Lidia directly and she may be able to persuade you to change your mind? You may not be safe, your friend may not be safe either."

This was compelling and reassuring that Diamond was not a lane dwelling seducer. "Can I think about it and get back to you?"

Their usual protocol kicked in. "If you give me an address you trust I will talk to Lidia and leave a message for you with details for a meeting in a few days."

They exchanged details and he advised he was staying to watch the stars. She suppressed the urge to comment and reached out to shake his hand. He seized the opportunity to unnecessarily graze her forearm.

"I know you won't tell me your name, so I won't ask, but I hope I see you again."

Electricity shot up her arm and, while she was caught off-guard, he leant down and kissed her cheek then broke away to settle back into his nonchalant stance against the shelter. She was trying desperately to be offended at his presumptuousness but the grin on her face betrayed her. She left, ignoring his eyes on her; turning her mind to whether to re-join the land and never look back.

8

Patrice was pleasantly surprised to find she had been assigned an apartment under the Dome. The building was designed to be locked down if an attack on Department Central required the Dome to take control of the City. In the event of a lockdown, a helicopter would retrieve her from wherever she was and drop her on the roof. The Chief Operator had arranged for her to practice the roof drop procedure at a training facility, so as not to draw attention to their location. She took comfort in the knowledge she would likely never have to jump onto the narrow roof surrounding the Dome while suspended in the air during a crisis, but nonetheless appreciated the lengths they had gone to in order to ensure she was prepared. The capability of the Dome was boundless and Patrice was perpetually in awe of her colleagues' fastidious planning.

During her orientation, they had explained why the Dome had been constructed after the Anniversary Attacks. Since formation, the Department Assembly and all essential services had been based at Department Central. The Department headquarters, known as Department Central, was located at the old Melbourne Central Shopping Centre. The block had been acquired after formation as it was the only site in the CBD which enabled direct access into a building from the City Loop underground train line. The renovation to convert the complex into a multidisciplinary government facility had taken years and the result was outstanding. Almost half a century later, the structure still dazzled. The train underneath enabled complete self-containment. Eventually, the City Loop was closed to citizens to guarantee secure direct access for Department Staff to travel between the various Department buildings spattered across the City.

In the years before the Anniversary Attacks, there had been a spate of phantom attacks on Department Central. Sympathisers were bypassing and tricking alarms all over the City. The attacks were faked in order to divert resources which were later revealed to have been groundwork for the Anniversary Attacks. At the time, there was no cause to suspect the malfunctions were connected. It was only after numerous failed deployments that the presumed defective triggers were discovered to have been deliberately activated. Countless reviews undertaken after the Anniversary Attacks highlighted the weaknesses and simple solutions to diversify and infuse inherent confirmation into systems were comprehensively implemented. One of the reviews had found many of the false alarms would have been able to be visually confirmed immediately had the need been previously envisaged; and recommended a covert facility be constructed at the top of a skyscraper.

The Department had scoured the City for the perfect building and all paled in comparison to one located at the north east corner of the CBD. The building was tall enough to enable views over the surrounding buildings but, at forty storeys, the Dome still had good visibility of the street level. Once the building was identified the Department had acquired all the office space. Given the Dome's disguise as a private rooftop garden within a greenhouse, a residential context drew less attention and the building was converted into a residential tower.

The old Parliament building and its gardens, Department East, had been converted into a research and development precinct once the governance staff had been relocated to Department Central after formation. The location of the Dome was central enough to have a direct view to Department Central to its west and directly down into Department East to its south.

Because the facility was required to act as an interim command centre after a disaster, the building also needed to be completely self-sufficient. The Dome's footprint was miniscule compared to all the levels of the building required to support its independence. Operation of all consoles required eighteen staff. In the event of a disaster, the building was designed to be able to be locked down for one year. Each post had a rotation of four specialist staff of which, at any one time, only one was able to be away from the building; in the event of a lockdown, the remaining three would be ready to fall into a daily rotation until the crisis was resolved. Since operation commenced, this rule had never been broken. Similarly, doctors, nurses and even a surgery had been built into the lower levels along with hydroponic labs for growing food, a kitchen and cooks for the entire staff.

Whenever Patrice arrived at the Dome on weekends, unlike the rest of the City, the pace and focus was as precise as any other day. The maintenance of the buildings' lockdown procedures and stocktake of supplies happened like clockwork once a month and took weeks to prepare. Once the drill had been run it was time to start planning the next one—this rotation the only semblance of regeneration within the Dome's unremitting consistency. For once, Patrice could not find any obvious inefficiency which had not been exploited. She was in the company of the finest servants. Their work immaculate and their professionalism flawless. The strict adherence to structure suited Patrice and the certainty their regiment provided made her task of learning their vast function quicker than expected.

Patrice had finished mastering what she considered to be the functional elements of the Dome and next wanted to familiarise herself with current threats. She had advised the Chief Operator of her intention for this visit and a monitor had been prepared for her, loaded with their top surveillance priorities.

9

Lidia's heart had stopped beating momentarily. Fortunately Diamond's behaviour was so outrageous, she was shocked back to life. His exuding onto this girl was so awkward she muted the feed and watched in silence as the ghost of her love sat patiently and stared at the water. As soon as April stepped into the frame, Lidia knew immediately she was Anna's niece. They were almost identical at that age which was unnerving and heartbreaking. It made sense April could have learned of Lidia's location from her father, while remaining unaware of the context.

When Anna died, April was four years old and the decision had been made to cut all communications permanently in order to keep her safe. April's father, Anna's brother, had been instrumental in allowing sympathisers access into Department South during the Anniversary Attacks. While he wasn't caught, he was never without suspicion. After Anna's death, he would certainly be under surveillance. As a result, Lidia knew nothing of April. She had not sought to follow her childhood, lest she were intercepted.

The meeting was short. Lidia watched mortified as Diamond kissed her and looked very happy with himself as she sprinted away. Thankfully, April was smiling. Lidia wasn't sure she would be able to regard him the same way after witnessing his alter ego and switched off the monitors. The audio had been recorded but Lidia didn't need to hear what they said. She returned to her window seat and waited for Diamond.

In the wake of Anna's slaughter, there had been discussions about whether the sympathisers should retaliate or wait to remerge. The trauma from the Anniversary Attacks was still fresh. Death had reverberated through their ranks and they'd withdrawn to take care of friends and families left behind. Struggling to accept the disproportional justice with no outlet for redress, they had stopped to regroup and regain their composure; nonetheless the resolve to continue to fight to return democracy was still potent. It was Lidia who resolutely enforced a hiatus. The regression was criticised as ridiculous but she had seen the Department's capacity for evil and knew their only chance would be to dissipate and fake extinction to allow time for new Department leaders to grow. Those who were instrumental in drafting the Formation Agreement – and equally effectual at extending its force indefinitely – were starting to move on from their posts. Still mentoring but passing the power on to their junior luminaries. Bred after formation, it was Lidia's hope that ignorance would be the Department's downfall, its emerging leaders unprepared for them in another era.

It was agreed there should be no communication and that Lidia, and a selection of survivors who would not be missed, would retreat permanently to the Lamasery and hibernate and prepare their resurgence. Everyone else was to forget them and move on with their lives. Emergency channels were established, kisses imprinted on bruised and bloodied cheeks and goodbyes reluctantly forced as allies parted, weak and broken. In the decade after Anna was killed, Lidia took no interest in the plans they had made. She felt dead also. Anna was her love completely and forever from the moment they had met to the moment she was viciously stolen; there would never be any person more perfect. The agony of the longing took years to relent. Others died and aged around her and her body, too, grew old while her heart remained still. In part, her indifference was coupled with the knowledge their plans were set and now her task was to wait.

Contrary to Lidia's expectations, however, the new Department leadership was more aggressive and more willing to punish and restrict than anyone anticipated. It seemed that, in the absence of opposition, these leaders only knew force and had no appreciation for governance. They lacked context and this disabled them. Unlike their predecessors, they did not even seek to maintain the pretext of the Formation Agreement and guzzled their authority with the greed of rulers—unfazed by their illegitimacy and determined to inflict their will despite necessity. It was this unabashed arrogance which Lidia suspected seeded the brewing contempt. She could see it on the faces of the people she watched from the window.

10

While designed to keep the City operating in the event of a significant attack on Department Central, the Dome was also tasked with monitoring threats to the City. Therefore any incident which impacted the threat level required Patrice urgently for briefings at the Dome. The threat level had not changed since Patrice joined the Department as a cadet after school. This was particularly relieving as – until he was elevated to the Department Assembly – she would be unable to tell her husband about this secret requirement of her portfolio. She expected he would not appreciate being abandoned if the City was attacked for weeks or months with no explanation or notice.

Threats to the City were not publicised unless it was absolutely necessary. As a result, Patrice wasn't surprised to have had limited knowledge of the current threats being monitored by the Dome. Patrice was in the age group which was most defensive of the Department. She had been a child when the Anniversary

Attacks took place and a teenager when the Court of Justice had been burnt down and was too young to remember life before the Department. From her viewpoint, having been blessed with a comfortable upbringing without the memory of democracy, the chaos and fear had emerged from nowhere. She was still, all these years later, unable to derive any purpose from their actions.

She remembered being terrified at the reactiveness of Anna's supporters in the wake of her death. Even in their grief and rage what purpose did destroying a building hold? What symbolism, other than to expose their own impetuousness, did this rebellion evoke? While the number of deaths following the Anniversary Attacks was sickening, they succeeded a judicial process which found that just as many people were innocent. The deaths were horrific, but the punishment was, in Patrice's mind, correlated to their own choices and actions. Contrastingly, burning down the Court was an act of violence against the people in the City. She could not reconcile this act which served to achieve nothing and took from the City an institution it treasured. This was the sentiment of most people born after formation—with the retraction of Lidia and other defenders of democracy, there were no alternative perspectives challenging their loyalty.

While Patrice was new to surveillance, her instinct doubted there could have been no fluctuations or thwarted attacks in a city of this size in decades. Once Patrice completed her review, she interviewed off-duty team members who had contributed to meticulously compiling the files and asked what, in aggregate, they derived from these observations. Not what the evidence showed, but what they felt. The files included groups who were mostly intimidating and sometimes violent, instigating crimes in their local areas. However, these groups were financially motivated and there was no suggestion there were any political causes underlying their anti-social activities.

Similarly the Dome monitored many individuals who had been prominent during the Anniversary Attacks but seemed now to be living normal lives. Patrice found, after several conversations with different officers, they had all formed the same conclusion. It was too clean. These people had no contact at all after being associated for years. They were never seen together. Never broke any rules. They were exceptionally well-behaved even when no one was watching. They never spoke about the future or the past. They were, in everyone's opinion, masking something.

She retired to her apartment to complete her initial review of the current threats and prepare the threat level status update, and compile a report of her key findings for the monthly meeting of the Department Assembly. She sat at her desk, people cheerfully picnicking in the park below, and contemplated the prospect of outwitting an invisible enemy. Having pondered her dilemma too long, Patrice decided to seek a private consultation with Secretary Clifton. She was advised by her predecessor it was normal to seek two to three private meetings per year. Any less would look like you weren't sufficiently aware of your portfolio and any more would seem needy. To date, she hadn't requested a meeting, and this was genuinely an issue on which she would appreciate his counsel.

11

The bar was pulsating to the beat and the crowd moved as one, hypnotised by the vibrations. April sat in the furthest booth from the door and absorbed their coordination. Diamond had informed her Lidia would meet her at the back of the bar. She had never sought to go dancing. It was frowned upon, like an admission of latent discontent. Observing their joy captivated by the music, it was hard to believe dancing was the gateway to anarchy. A hooded figure slid into the booth obscuring her view of the dance floor. April refocused her eyes in the dark to find Lidia sitting opposite her. She was an older version of the girl in the history books, however she didn't move like an old woman. She was nimble and fast. Pulling back the hood, Lidia held back her tears.

"I'm Lidia, you must be April." Lidia held out her hand. Startled at the recognition, April panicked, aware she was, literally, cornered. "Don't be frightened. I knew your father."

Questions too many to grasp inundated April's mind. "How do you know my father?"

"I was married to his sister. Your aunt, Anna. I'm your aunt." Lidia couldn't contain her emotions and tears spilled down her face.

April, stunned, interrogated the proposition. "My father doesn't have a sister."

"This is not a conversation we can have here tonight, I don't have much time. I came to tell you not to speak of this to anyone especially not your father. He is monitored by the Department. I will send word to him you have found me and I will teach you about your aunt in a safe place. Now tell me, who told you about the Lamasery?"

Too flustered to disobey, April blurted the truth. "It was a story he told me as a kid but it seemed real, then I overheard someone at work saying you were alive. I wondered if it was true, so I did some snooping and found love letters from someone who lived at the Lamasery."

Lidia was impressed. Clever girl just like Anna. The love letters were an anagram. Each emergency channel had a different key and the letter's sign off advised Lidia which key she needed to decipher the code within the letter. Over the years, Lidia had received sporadic letters from April's father when relatives died or on Anna's birthday. Nothing regular and nothing which, if intercepted, would be incriminating. There was no time to explain the necessary precautions of a covert existence.

"When will you see your father next?"

"We have dinner on Wednesdays."

"I will get word to him before then. Do not say anything to him about your investigation. Go back to your normal life and

I will have Diamond organise our next meeting in a month from now."

Lidia smiled softly, replaced her hood and left out a rear door.

12

Secretary Clifton's office in Department Central was, unusually, on the ground floor. He liked to be close to the train station and his office had a view of the lobby where he could discreetly watch over the staff. He'd found, over the years, that Department Managers were too distant from their subordinates and often too busy to effectively detect undercurrents of discontent in their ranks; and a few of them cared less than he would have liked about the culture of support he had carried on from Chen. This culture was the cornerstone of the Department's ability to maximise efficiencies as these innovations were often driven by the staff.

Secretary Chen had been appointed the first Department Secretary and had been patently superlative to her colleagues. She didn't tolerate subordination. Anyone not completely dedicated to service of the Department was dismissed. The Department Assembly had disbanded with lengthy and convoluted laws after formation and instead the Governance Rules employed a simple mission: *Our people are free from fear and free from stress.* It was extremely effective. Years of slogans, meaningless words and empty actions had left even the most dedicated servants depleted and the mission revitalised the staff, enabling them to focus their actions and act to restore people's faith in their ability. Teams focused on the wellbeing of their citizens without having to consider the financial implications of their decisions which were solely the purview of the Department Managers. This ensured Department Mangers were genuinely accountable to Chen for their outputs and had nowhere to hide; if they weren't minimising spending aggressively and proactively they were demoted. Chen liked to remind her Department Managers 'poverty-stricken communities don't get second chances when we make mistakes so why should you?' Her priority was to get the City back to a respectable position and she expected excellence from every person. Anything less would not be tolerated.

The Department Assembly had fifty-nine members: fifty-eight Department Managers and the Department Secretary. Unlike Premiers of the past, the Secretary while superior was not the face of the Department. The role was akin to an elder or a mediator—a final decision-maker. The Department Assembly decided most things by vote; where there was no clear majority, the responsible Department Manager would make the final decision. When the decision was contentious, the Department Secretary would intervene and resolve the issue. Secretary Clifton had been appointed shortly after Anna had died. This was seen as a gesture to the City that their discontent at Anna's execution had been received although, in practicality, Secretary

Chen had been approaching eighty and frailty had begun to diminish her stamina. Clifton was popular. Chen's assistant in the years before her retirement, he had been elected almost unanimously and was regarded as profoundly well-reasoned. He also radiated wisdom which gave the Department Assembly confidence in his guidance, regardless of any evidence that this demeanour produced exemplary decision-making. Nonetheless, he was respected and trusted and his competence had strengthened their belief in his leadership.

The Department Managers had been given resources and autonomy but many within the Department Assembly recognised it was Chen's leadership which had facilitated their early success. However, while the task of the Department was to ensure people had a basic standard of living, it had not been anticipated that the provocation of debate and the capacity to transform, once removed, would also vanquish the soul of the City. The temporary resolution to establish order had diminished creativity. The City was less animated than it had been. With the will of the people supplanted, only the will of the Department Assembly remained. Nonetheless, the citizens whose lives had been awful prior to formation, having obtained a better standard of living, were unwilling to risk digression. As a result, in the years before the Department Assembly's expiry, tensions mounted creating rifts between the citizens who wanted to revert to democracy and the citizens who wanted the Department to remain. The Department Assembly, however unsolicited, had in its competence garnered its own supporters.

13

April was almost at work, climbing the steps up to Department East, when her mind randomly took her back to the bar where she met Lidia. She remembered the bodies crushed up against each other and the cries of delight when the song changed, then Diamond's lips on her cheek on the Pier, then the rush of adrenaline as the crates tumbled betraying her location in the lane. She couldn't deny, before that night, there had been something missing. Lidia wanted to meet again and while April did not want to become involved in her world, she was curious about Lidia's motivations.

The revelation she had an aunt and the subsequent closeness she felt to her father brought April peace. After the meeting, April had waited pensively at her childhood home. When the door opened, her father pulled her into a ferocious embrace and she felt, for the first time, his suppressed grief rise to the surface. Not only had he lost Anna, he had lost his identity.

She squeezed his hand and he winked at her and they sat down for dinner, relaxed in the knowledge he has a sister. April had, with hindsight, felt the void her whole life. Unable to identify the cause of her suspicions, deception had become the norm. There was congruence now; a level of respect for her father she had previously been unable to attain.

It was almost a month since she had met Lidia and her initial interest had dissipated. The hole in the fabric had been mended and she felt no desire to learn more from Lidia about the life she had chosen. Initially, April scoured the archives and read every historical article about Anna she was able to find. However, as Anna was so young when she had been incarcerated, many of the writings were about her potential and her icon not about her actual life. Nevertheless, the picture of Anna portrayed was one of unparalleled determination and fierce passion for her City and the freedom she cherished. She was a professional athlete and had been known globally for her advocacy for democracy which she amplified through her competitions. April – apparently a duplicate of her aunt – examined herself in comparison and, while similarly curious, was unable to identify any cause she would risk her life to defend.

April learned about the Formation Agreement at school. By then, the Department Assembly had been appointed in perpetuity and the history books had been adjusted. April knew this because she had found texts from the years immediately after formation when researching an assignment and they extensively referenced the need for stability through a tumultuous time in technological development. She had asked her father what he remembered from that time, as the differences between accounts were cavernous. Enlightened by current events, April realised he had taken her to a noisy football match to share his insights. She remembered it was his view that none of the later accounts reflected what was actually happening in the decade before formation.

Governments in the past had been primarily responsible for collecting taxes and redistributing resources. As technology advanced and information sharing made enormous amounts of information available, discontent emerged in every area of public discourse. Unfettered access to data resulted in prolific wastage of resources by politicians trying to maintain civility while being continuously undermined by disagreements over the veracity of basic facts. Eventually, as the number of discontented people became unmanageable, polarisation prevented consensus on basic issues like housing, water and food and the lower classes became impoverished. The indignity of poverty forced the leaders of all the political parties to come together and, as one, commit to a period of restitution whereby one government would be formed with the sole purpose of restoring civility.

Community leaders such as Anna were mortified that debates contesting ideas would be disbanded in favour of efficiency and that art and sport would be deferred because a small number of politicians could not adequately provide rudimentary services. Anna demanded to know why the entire City should suffer because of the ineptitudes of these unimaginative panicked Luddites. Many saw her as an idealist and challenged her to make a positive contribution to help alleviate the poverty instead of wasting resources on non-essentials. Anna was unrelenting, challenging officials at every chance, screaming at her fellow citizens, compelling them to look into their hearts and find the courage to stand up for the traditions and values of exploring humanity and individual expression and the variety in each of them which made their City the envy of the world. Her pleas were useless in the face of death, the sick and the starving.

By all accounts, even April's father's, the first few years after formation united the City and the sincerity of the mission – once Anna was conveniently indisposed – enabled the Department Assembly. One decade on, Secretary Chen's leadership had transformed the City and her strict management had elevated the impoverished back to an acceptable standard of living. It was her father's recollection that calls subsequently began for the Department Assembly to remain. However, the Anniversary Attacks thwarted the momentum; no one knew what might have happened if the decision had been deferred to the people.

April reached the top of the steps and considered the exquisite details in the tiles, for the first time imagining what this glorious building must have been like, chambers rattling to the chorus of agreement and dissent.

14

Clifton was sitting at his office window watching an exchange between two junior engineers. It appeared from their bright red faces, bloodshot eyes and inappropriate touching, that they were mid-tiff. His concentration broke as Patrice knocked on the door. He buzzed her in and invited her to sit at the desk. She looked tired and nervous. He pitied the time these brilliant minds worried over meetings with him.

"Patrice, I have been looking forward to our first meeting. I have heard from my liaisons with the Chief Operator you are in your element at the Dome. Do you agree with his assessment?"

She was slightly taken aback as he was looking out the window watching an argument in the lobby, smiling while talking to her; tranquil semi-focus was nonetheless preferable to being scolded.

"Thank you for the opportunity to accept this important work. I have been, so far, completely captivated by the team and their professionalism. It is a challenge at the Dome I have come to speak with you about, Secretary."

He turned to face her. He could hear the apprehension in her voice and was intrigued. He'd found with new Department Managers that it look a while before they developed a sense of when to escalate an issue to him. They usually referred matters between themselves to solve issues. He was typically called upon to advise on interpersonal issues where a decision may have an impact on someone else in the Department Assembly or they needed the impartiality and privacy of his perspective.

"I have thought about this issue at length and, as I am new to this portfolio, I would be grateful for your insights on operations at the Dome." He nodded for her to proceed. "I have been reviewing our current surveillance priorities and, at surface level, they are unconnected. I have spoken with the team and they have confirmed my suspicion—the absence of any overlap is in itself suspicious. When I queried the officers they were worried there was something they were missing. Essentially, they all agreed the behaviour they are observing is too deliberate. One said 'too good to be true'."

He had turned back to watching the argument, allowing himself a moment of pride in Patrice; this was exactly the type of issue he would expect her to bring to him.

"It sounds Patrice, like you are completely on top of things and have identified a weakness in the Dome's perhaps outdated clinical approach. A poignant observation." He had thought as much for some time and knew she would come to this conclusion. It was her uncanny talent for filtering out the noise which made her perfect for this type of work. She didn't need coddling; he appreciated she must be genuinely stuck. "So what is your plan now?"

She hesitated. He could see she knew what she wanted to do and needed a sounding board in case she had missed a critical consideration. He assumed it was hard on her not being able to talk to her husband about this element of her new portfolio. They were a team in every sense but it was nice to see her realising her strengths independently, space to shine.

"I want to interview the subjects myself. I am aware some of these people have been under surveillance for years, even decades, but I think we need to shake things up or we are going to be blindsided. I was looking back at the reviews undertaken after the Anniversary Attacks and the reports all referenced a malaise in the year before the attack. If we are seeing what they want us to see, or if they are making things neat to soothe us into believing there is nothing happening, maybe it's time we forced them to talk to us?"

He accepted this was a considered and researched plan but if she was completely certain she wouldn't have come to him. "What is your hesitation, Patrice? What are the risks of this approach?"

She knew what she thought might happen based on their personalities. "I am concerned they will go underground. At least now we can track them. They may be behaving defensively but they don't know definitively we are watching them. Also they haven't been charged with anything. We have permanent surveillance on Anna's associates and – while none ever gave us cause for suspicion – based on their behaviour, they clearly believe they are being watched. Further, this itself is not evidence they are actually planning something. I am concerned contact may motivate them, give them a reason to retaliate."

Her introspections were always a treat. These concerns were valid however he agreed, given recent history, the benefits outweighed the risks. They continued to discuss advantages and disadvantages of strategies and Patrice felt the pressure melt and her usual excitement for work return. They agreed on a strategy and Clifton gave his approval, absorbing the responsibility, so that she could commit fully to executing their plan.

15

Lidia was expecting Diamond shortly to discuss arrangements for her first visit with April; she was deciphering letters while she waited. It had been a productive month, meeting April had been revitalising. Part of her planning was ensuring those involved had the temperament for non-violent intervention. Lidia had not taken part in the Anniversary Attacks. She was not active with the sympathisers at the time; all of whom had later been sentenced to death. She had been with them in the beginning but became concerned with their methods and, eventually, withdrew her support. On that night she had made sure she was in attendance at the symphony so as not to be able to be associated with their violence.

After formation, people believed the sympathisers were fighting for freedom but lost faith in their moral righteousness after they burnt down the Court of Justice. From the outset, Lidia knew the only path to success was one where no blood was shed. Had she not been in shock, debilitated by grief, she would have been sentient to prevent the savagery. The trust the sympathisers lost retaliating was equal to the trust the Department Assembly lost killing Anna. In the aftermath, Lidia sensed resignation, and, fatigued, people retreated into their own lives and became further withdrawn from contributing to their communities.

The residual detachment and disinterest which settled that day was starting to thaw. The younger generations, having been spared these experiences, brought with them into adulthood renewed optimism their City could be even more wonderful. She allowed this hope into her heart; she'd always believed democracy could be restored and for the first time she felt others driving the change.

Diamond let himself in and sat at the table waiting for her to finish applying the code. When she looked up his face was plastered with doubt. She hadn't seen him like this before. Her heartrate quickened. "Spit it out."

He looked like he didn't want to be having this conversation. "I have a message for you." He was worried this would be the last message he delivered. He had uncharacteristically sat on the information for a few days wishing it was someone else who'd had the misfortune to be asked to deliver it. "The Department has requested a meeting with you. They say they were made aware you were alive after a recent visit to the dentist. They want to know where you have been since Anna died."

Shocked but not surprised, Lidia had no doubt they knew exactly where she was but it was interesting they were reaching out to her now. Something had changed. Only one way to find out what. "Where do they want to meet?"

"A woman called Patrice says she can meet you anytime or any place which suits you. The message was that she will have personal security but that the meeting will not be monitored. She just wants to talk."

Lidia laughed. She doubted very much this woman wanted to talk. She was probably trying to prove a theory. It was impossible they could have learned of their plans as Lidia was the only person who was aware of all the elements; stored securely in her head. Over the years, different sympathisers had emerged and tried to make contact to collaborate, and she always declined, contritely explaining since Anna's death she had moved on. She assumed these characters would not have been deterred by her rejection but hoped, however, they had the decency not to glamourise violence. Regardless, the Department was sophisticated in its interruption of such deviances as evidenced by the extended period of calm.

Her heart rate returned to normal. "I assume you look nervous because I'm going to ask you how the Department was able to get to me through you?"

"Um, yes."

"I also assume you don't know?" He shook his head.

"It was through a mate. Her brother works for a Department Manager. They were asking their staff if anyone knew you because they needed your help. He fell for it. I have known them since we were kids. It wouldn't have occurred to him it might be a trap. He's a sweet guy. He thought he was being helpful."

"Do you think it's a trap?"

He sighed and slumped in his chair. "If they were going to kill you they probably wouldn't be telling you about it. If they had any evidence they would just arrest you. I don't know. I want to believe they need your help."

"You have clearly thought about this for a while." She could see he was pained. At least he wasn't being sloppy. Many people knew Department employees and sympathisers were, if not inciting rebellion, not expected to hide their opposition to the Department Assembly. This type of entanglement made it necessary for them to maintain the containment strategy. It would be too easy for the Department to track her if she tried to live a normal life. She considered the invitation.

"I will meet with them. I agree with your assessment. I doubt they need my help, I suspect they're fishing." She gave him a reassuring smile. "Let's try and find out what they really want."

16

Patrice spent the morning baking tarts and arranging an assortment of fruit, salmon and prawn canapes; their decadent dining room was set for two. Entertaining was an expectation of Department Managers who often hosted dignitaries.

All Department Managers were offered an estate for their tenure and their residences were used by the Department to conduct business in the regions. Given her and her husband's prospects within the Department, they had been offered Rippon Lea Estate. After formation, Local Councils remained with Department appointed community leaders to make decisions on local matters. Department Managers, in addition to their portfolios, were expected to be available to advise and support the Local Councillors. As a result, their estates were cherished by their communities and they often used the grounds for celebrations and ceremonies.

Patrice decided if she wasn't going to treat Lidia like a criminal, she would welcome her as she would any other community leader. This brunch was the typical scale expected of a meeting between a Department Manager and person who was held locally in high esteem. Given Lidia had never been arrested, Patrice felt it prudent to afford her the appropriate level of respect. Having studied her profile, she was in awe of Lidia and was interested to learn how she had maintained her resolve. The immaculate house was embellished with freshly cut flowers. Patrice took a few moments to prepare her covert attire, ready to head directly to the Dome to debrief once Lidia left.

The gravel crunched outside and Patrice raced down the stairs to greet Lidia on the verandah. She stood taller than Patrice had expected and looked hyperalert and sceptical.

"Welcome to Rippon Lea, Lidia." She reached out and shook her hand as Lidia, distracted, scanned her surroundings. "Before brunch let me take you on a quick tour of the estate." Lidia smiled politely and thanked Patrice for the kind offer. She wasn't interested in the slightest but assumed this ritual was a stencil of Department etiquette, and obliged.

She enjoyed the tour, the pretence giving her time to gain her composure. The last stop was the security room and Lidia caught a glimpse of the real Patrice.

"Lidia, as I promised, this meeting will not be recorded." Patrice pointed to the monitor displaying the dining room and controls for the cameras and microphones and switched them off, then advised her security she had prepared brunch for them in the garden. Silky diplomacy. Lidia found herself warming to this woman in spite of her staunch and complete mistrust.

Patrice ended the tour in the dining room, took her seat and invited Lidia to coffee, filled their plates and discarded with the pleasantries.

"Thank you for meeting with me. As you would expect the Department has a kept an eye on your movements over the years."

Lidia was relieved this woman wasn't going to waste their time pretending the Department wanted to ask her where she'd been all this time.

"Lidia, I hope you understand our surveillance is precaution-ary and do not take offence." Lidia shook her head. She wasn't offended. She expected nothing less.

"I must admit when I started to read your file I wasn't expect-ing to be impressed by your commitment and affection for those who looked to you for leadership after Anna's incarceration. You accepted that responsibility and sought to influence her follow-ers for peaceful reintroduction of democracy and, from what I have been able to ascertain, have not faltered."

The flattery was transparent. Lidia's face was blank while waiting for the reason she'd been summoned to be revealed. "Why am I here, Patrice?"

"I expected you may be impatient with the formalities but I hope you will oblige me. Having prepared for this meeting, there is something I would first like to clarify. During the Anniversary Attacks, you reported the location of an explosive device which we, as a result, were able to intercept. Had it reached its destina-tion thousands more would have died."

Lidia blushed. She was not aware anyone knew that had been her. Patrice was correct.

"At the time the Department decided not to pursue your defection. You had gone to great lengths to avoid detection and concerns regarding retaliation were prioritised. The details of this foiled plot were never released."

Lidia had wondered why no one had come for her blood after that night.

"We, at the Department, consider you as an ally. Although I doubt you reciprocate the sentiment."

She thought about this. Lidia didn't consider the Department as her enemy but the hegemony they veiled certainly. Politely, she moved them forward from platitudes. "Thank you for your candour, Patrice. You are testing my patience."

Patrice acknowledged the criticism apologetically. "I invited you into my home because you are clearly not a threat to this City. I suspect you have dissuaded many rowdy sympathises from pursuing their aggression in your time. So, why are you hiding?"

Touché. Lidia smiled. Such duplicity to be enjoying this pleasant brunch in the company of a scintillating woman. Refreshing to be asked the right question. "I'm not hiding."

"If you aren't hiding then what are you doing? Because you aren't living. You are never seen walking or eating or shopping. You are only ever seen in emergencies. Am I to believe you are just anti-social?"

She shrugged. "You can believe whatever you like."

"Or I can believe what the evidence tells me. You are planning another revolution."

"And if I were, Patrice, would you expect me to tell you? Do you serve all the terrorists your finest caviar?"

Patrice laughed. She had chosen to be completely honest with Lidia and this honesty had been repaid. She was undoubtedly planning something. "Only the nice ones."

They both laughed.

"Lidia, I respect that your beliefs as to the governance of our City differ from mine. I also respect your commitment to preserving life and dissuading violence, common values we both share. However I did ask you here for your help. You may deplore violence but there are sympathisers emerging who do not share your constitution. Most people believe you are dead. If you would come out of hiding perhaps your re-emergence would give such sympathisers somewhere to focus their attention—someone who would be a responsible influence."

Lidia considered this suggestion. Diamond had warned of a trap. She needed time.

"Let me think about it, Patrice. You might need to offer me more than salmon."

17

In the years after Anna's death, Lidia didn't dare visit her grave. The ruse she herself had also passed away was vital to their plans and many of Anna's followers still visited to pay their respects; she would have been recognised. After meeting Patrice, Lidia's overwhelming urge was not to indulge her advice or cancel their plans but to be with Anna. Patrice was charming, however Lidia was unconvinced the proposition was so straight forward. It seemed unlikely the Department was trying to appoint a leader for sympathisers to follow. More likely they'd become aware of a dangerous threat and she was the lesser evil. Perhaps the Department, like Lidia, had sensed there was growing appetite for change and decided it was time for democracy to be reinstated.

The cemetery was enormous. Fortunately, the destination was popular with tourists and her request for directions was not conspicuous. Once she found the plot, Lidia waited nearby for a break in the worshippers and was, at last, reunited with her wife. Anna's family had arranged the funeral and the gravestone read: loving wife, daughter, and sister. Strangers were disappointed at the simplicity of this sentiment. While people knew her for her sportsmanship and advocacy, it was her family she loved most fiercely. She was blessed with natural ability and her drive was insatiable; the adoration of her community pushed her to strive for perfection and motivated her to maintain the punishing physicality of her craft. Lidia ran her hands over the worn stone and pressed her fingers into the dirt. Crippled with grief, she lay on the grass, the ache in her heart and bones ubiquitous. So few moments after so many years. But Anna was not there and Lidia peeled herself off the ground and lugged her limp body back to the shadows.

Lidia stayed for another hour before she felt ready to leave. She watched the faces of Anna's visitors and the tears and smiles and wondered what Anna would have done in Lidia's position. Patrice was inviting Lidia to be the leader Anna was born to be, but to lead them where? Anna would have taken them without hesitation to the Secretary's front door, demanding his attention or something equally as provocative. Lidia was never as evocative as Anna but perhaps that was what Patrice wanted. Anna, upon release, ignited the City's determination to reclaim its former identity; that had got her killed. So why now? Was it possible Patrice hadn't considered what would likely happen if Lidia revealed herself to be alive? Anna's devotees would undoubtedly interpret her return as a signal that time had come for resurgence.

She left the cemetery and proceeded to an abandoned building where Diamond was waiting to take her to a safehouse; they would wait for a week or two before returning to the Lamasery in case the Department was tracking her. These weeks away also allowed her to visit with the few people who were aware she was still alive. This time, with April.

Once they'd unpacked and Diamond showed her the security procedures, Lidia told him about her meeting with Patrice. He would not normally be privy to this type of operational detail but given it was his life which had been infiltrated she felt he deserved to have his curiosity satisfied, albeit vaguely.

Diamond's inclination toward the audacious had started to attract him to mischief before he was old enough to know better; his role supporting Lidia aptly suited his furtiveness and had kept him out of actual trouble. Since becoming infatuated with April he had been insufferable. He had somehow conjured their love story from what Lidia guessed was a total of around five minutes together and he was desperate to see her again. Nonetheless, she hadn't told him April was her niece. It was danger enough April knew the truth but with the Department now connected to Diamond she had to be additionally cautious with him.

She cooked them dinner and told him as they ate about Rippon Lea Estate and Patrice's suggestion she formalise her leadership. She asked him if, in light of their original message, he still thought their motives disingenuous.

"The only reason they would want you to lead us out in the open is if they think you're already leading us in secret."

Her thoughts exactly.

"Why would they want to do that?"

"Because they don't know how many of us are following you." Correct again. He was sceptical. "Did she say what she wants you to actually do, other than tell people you are still alive? They killed Anna."

Anna died before he was born but Diamond spoke her name like it hurt him to remember her death. She hadn't pressed Patrice on the semantics nor a reason or a timeframe. They were sizing each other up. It was not the time for details.

"What do you think, Diamond. Are you sick of living two lives?"

He scrunched his nose in thought. "I don't want them to kill you. They can't kill you if you're already dead."

Seemingly falling in lust had turned Diamond into a puddle. Seldom sentimental, his concern for her was touching. She had not sought this opportunity nor could they force her to change her lifestyle but it was to the Department's advantage she remain disappeared—if an undercurrent of discontent was swelling, her return would be a catalyst. Regardless, decisions would need to be made. She could proceed with her plans. She could accept the offer to work with the Department. She couldn't do nothing.

Diamond washed the dishes while Lidia organised her week. She had a busy schedule of meetings relating to the operation of the Lamasery and Anna's Estate. She felt different. The futility of her attempted concealment relaxed her and the admission by Patrice that the Department considered her fondly was surprisingly comforting although she suspected she had been spared the implicit disclaimer.

Lidia was exhausted and her heart was tired. Decisions could wait. She was looking forward to her time with April.

18

Not one for ruminating, Patrice found her new responsibilities at the Dome forced her to double and triple check her work. Doubting herself was unfamiliar, however the weight of the responsibility she now carried required her to be more careful than with past portfolios. She found her Dome apartment to be an excellent retreat to rankle at strategies.

In order to minimise the possibility Patrice was inside Department Central in a crisis, her office had been relocated to Department East next to the Dome. The covert methods employed to enter the facility required an exaggerated detour but, nonetheless, knowing she was close to her office if her staff needed her helped her concentrate.

She had stumbled upon a curious coincidence and wasn't sure whether it was a good use of her time to have it pursued. Patrice learned after their brunch Lidia visited Anna's grave. The report had highlighted how raw Lidia's grief was, so many decades after Anna's death. Lidia's profile listed immediate family but not Anna's family as Anna was alive and her file active when the profile had first been complied. Patrice requested the Dome include Anna's connections and swiftly Lidia's file was updated with details of all Anna's immediate and extended family, through to second cousins.

When she examined the list Patrice immediately recognised April's name. She walked past her office regularly. She was a statistician in Department East. Patrice often passed her in the halls; she was well regarded by her Department Manager. As Lidia was widely presumed to be dead, Patrice was unsure whether Anna's family were aware she was still alive. Lidia's profile indicated she had spent a considerable amount of time with her own mother before she died but there was no indication Lidia had any contact with her in-laws after Anna died; in particular with Anna's brother whom Lidia was known to have been close. The intelligence indicated April was not involved with sympathisers and her father also worked at the Department. Nevertheless, the past few weeks had taught her the intelligence was potentially flawed. Patrice was due to head home. Her husband had sensed something was troubling her and wanted to take her out for dinner. Instead she decided to drop by April's office and see if she could gauge whether there was more to her than her than the file portrayed.

People had started leaving for the day, however she could see through the window to April's office that her light was still on. It was odd someone so junior had an office on this side of the building. The door was ajar and Patrice could see through the sliver; April was deep in concentration fixated on something she was deconstructing on a whiteboard. She didn't want to startle her but it was possible April may be standing there for another hour so she rapped her nails gently on the door. April gasped and spun around, and then gasped again when she saw Patrice.

"Hello Madam, please come in. Would you like a seat?" April frantically grabbed books off the chairs opposite her desk and stuffed them into draws and overfull bookshelves. Patrice didn't intend on staying for more than a minute but felt obliged to take a seat given her trouble.

"Hi April. Please, call me Patrice. How are you?"

April fell onto her chair, starstruck. "I'm well. Thank you. I was just trying to solve an equation. How can I help you?"

While Patrice was now located in the building, April was not working directly for her on any projects. Regardless it wasn't unusual for Department Managers to ask questions, particularly of technical staff, if they were trying to determine whether there was an efficiency to be gained by collaborating. It was like having a celebrity drop into your office. April was too shocked to be nervous. This was exactly what Patrice was hoping, to catch her unexpectedly so there was no time for her to prepare if there was something she wanted to hide. Given she was completely flustered, Patrice was satisfied there was nothing sinister about her appointment.

"I was hoping to quickly see whether you had any interest in the Accelerated Junior Leadership Program. We have a few more places available and your work has been noticed by your Department Manager. I am coordinating the program for Department East and, I don't want to pressure you, but I think you have a bright future at the Department."

April had been thinking about it but with all the chaos in her life had completely forgotten to complete the application.

Patrice didn't want to seem too deliberate. She was mindful that if April had spoken to Lidia recently, this visit may seem like an attempt to get to Lidia through her family which was not the intention. Patrice stood up and hurried to the door.

"I've got a handful of other potential candidates to visit tonight so I've got to keep moving but get in touch if you want more details. Applications close end of next week." As a precaution she dropped in on a few others in case April asked if anyone else had received personal encouragement then headed directly to the restaurant.

They had a beautiful dinner. After over a decade together, it never ceased to amaze her how she could fall even more in love with him. He knew her completely. When she was stressed he knew she was working through something and that he was her escape; if she wanted his advice she would ask him for it and if she didn't, it was his job to make her laugh. He knew he was the love of her life and he never doubted her or confused her stress with work for discontent in their relationship and she felt exactly the same toward him. Their time together was precious and on nights they dedicated to each other, the world around them faded away and she re-emerged energised ready to tackle whatever problems she'd deferred with renewed enthusiasm.

At dinner she was excited to hear he had been approached to interview for two different Department Manager roles. Appointments took years at that level. Matching the person to the role depended on considering their experience, location and other commitments, such as conflicts with Patrice's work. They'd had a loose plan since they got engaged that they would start trying to get pregnant once both had been promoted to Department Manager. There were several married couples in the Department Assembly and they tended to have sensitive or security portfolios. She assumed this was to enable the person not to be alienated from their partner. She couldn't think of worse timing but she trusted Secretary Clifton and was certain the possibility of children would have been discussed; she wouldn't be able to jump out of a helicopter.

She couldn't wait to tell her husband what she had been working on, particularly when she was constantly having to lie about trivial things such as how the security cameras just happened to malfunction at the exact same time she had a friend over for brunch, but only in one room. Their reconnection was imminent. On the trip home, spent from laughing, she pondered how such perfection could exist in one person.

19

Lidia had a revealing week consulting on Patrice's motives with her network. While perpetually strategising, their plans had never literally considered the Department. Diamond was worried the Department were planning to round up all the sympathisers, lull them into a false sense of security and then kill them. Her advisors doubted they were actually planning anything at all. There was no indication from anyone's sources the Department Assembly was either feeling threatened, concerned about an uprising or planning to reinstate democracy. They suspected Patrice was acting on her own and trying to genuinely, as she had said, figure out why Lidia was in hiding. Their insights were invaluable and over the years, they had proved mostly to be accurate in their assessments of these tactile matters.

Interestingly however, their advice differed vastly when she asked them what they thought she should do next. Some advised to cut contact, others said to take the opportunity to negotiate with the Department, others said to use the relationship to her advantage to gain information but to continue her plans unaffected. She would have preferred consensus on a strategy moving forward. Regardless, their misalignment reinforced the potential for miscalculation and the need for caution.

She'd spent the day worrying over whether to tell April about her plans. She wanted to be able to have a real relationship with her niece. Without context, this wouldn't be possible. She was aware, however, that April had told Diamond when he arranged their visit that she didn't want to be involved in Lidia's plans; she only wanted to get to know her aunt. How to explain to April that her plans were a part of her? From Lidia's perspective everything else was suspended until this work was done.

Her evening with April had been pleasant but her niece was struggling to accept Lidia's absent yet intimate role in her life, and was overwhelmed. April had drawn the conclusion Lidia had chosen her rebellion over her family. Lidia having never heard her choice expressed as such was upset. Factually, that correlation was accurate, however April did not understand that for Lidia there was no choice. Completing Anna's work, defending their values, making the sacrifices she had were never deliberate or considered; they were as concrete as the floor under them. Not once had not fighting for a return to freedom been even a seed in her mind. April, though, only saw the time they didn't spend together, the secrets kept from her, the lie her father was forced to live. Lidia excruciatingly accepted that in April's mind her choices were selfish and tenderly sought to repair some of the damage she had caused by focusing on April's childhood and her hopes for the future.

Listening to April's stories without Anna's memory was painful but Lidia was reassured in the knowledge Anna would have preferred her to be safe. In time, Lidia hoped April would want to learn more about the world Anna had once defended. She was hopeful eventually she would have the opportunity to convince her niece that the life she was living was subdued in comparison to the life she could have. April wasn't ready for that conversation, she needed time to be hurt and angry. Lidia was conflicted as she listened to April's love for her work. Like many who worked for the Department they were raised in a time where the Department was the only avenue for certain professions, particularly in statistical analysis. Lidia listened for inclinations, subtly leading questions to ascertain whether April's devotion was to the Department or maths. April had recently submitted an application for a leadership program and was excited at the prospect of being selected. She enjoyed being close to the seminar chambers at Department East where Department Managers would host experts and researchers; she would regularly sneak in to eavesdrop on different disciplines curious about the ways their work intersected. She was ambitious but not for herself; she appreciated the opportunities afforded to her to achieve and excel. She was exactly like Anna. How remarkable her temperament matched precisely that of an aunt she never knew existed. Contrastingly, April had less than no interest in physical competition but their drive and focus were indistinguishable.

Diamond had offered to escort April home. He had been instructed to take the evening off but insisted he would wait outside to ensure they were safe. Lidia had conceded she would not be able to keep him away from April and decided to explain their familial connection. He was blown away and, before he could stop himself, he exclaimed if he married her they would be family. She wondered whether infatuation was able to be weaponised. April had been excited to see Diamond also but was obviously not equally obsessed. Lidia was not looking forward to April's crush expiring and having to deal with a shattered Diamond and hoped his feelings would dissipate as rapidly as they had formed.

Lidia's time away from the Lamasery was almost concluded and once alone again after her treasured interlude with April she deliberated over packing. Their plans, decades in the making, had been more or less in place for some years. At her age, she understood the flow of this City. She had witnessed before the nexus where people dared to want for more in their lives and the trickle slowly became a flood. Lidia was waiting for the trickle to expand.

This interjection from Patrice, however, offered the opportunity for a completely different kind of revolution—uniquely sanctioned by the Department. One of the ways in which the Department had been able to maintain its authority unchallenged was through championing local issues; Department Managers were apt at directing the talents of ambitious people. The Department had never sought to silence people with opinions—only identify and harness that energy to its advantage. As a result, unanticipated conflict was rare. Lidia wondered whether she should seize Patrice's naivety and push for a negotiation, aware she was the only one with the knowledge to execute their plans. If Lidia was arrested or killed, there was no one who could take her place.

20

Mindful not to undermine Patrice, Clifton had requested to be kept informed of her progress in person. He had advised her to keep her inquiries between them until they had been able to ascertain whether there was any connection between the individuals the Dome had been following. Patrice, after interviewing each separately, was not concerned they were working together but was left with the sense their support networks were more expansive than the Dome had been aware. She had enjoyed meeting their surveillance subjects. All but Lidia had criminal convictions and she had the Police organise their interviews under the pretext of seeking information about an associate; she was not concerned the setting would offend them. They were not coy. They were blunt in their disdain for the Department but she didn't detect any moral or philosophical objection, most of them were not old enough to be able to remember life before the Department. Contrarian for the sake of it she surmised, but even so, if pitted against authority, they could be rallied.

As she updated Clifton, he sat in thought contemplating their next step.

"Patrice, your work has been impeccable. Remind me, how did you leave things with Lidia?"

"She wanted time to consider my proposal that she come out of hiding. I didn't push for a response. She's smart. I suspect she is planning something. She has a reason for faking her death but she won't tell me what it is yet."

He nodded. "In concert with all you have learned, do you think she will reach out to you again?"

"She may. Her niece works in Department East, but I don't think she knows Lidia is alive. I don't want to have to use that against her." She frowned at the thought.

"No, and I wouldn't ask you to, Patrice. If she comes to you and wants to come out of hiding, what were you planning on preparing to substantiate her absence? If your strategy is that we manage her return because it is less likely to result in an uprising of these discontented people, do you have a task for her to perform?"

She had thought broadly about this. Lidia had a motivation for staying hidden all these years. Without knowing what inspired her, crafting a proposition was problematic. More than their repartee over brunch, Lidia's diversion to Anna's grave had given Patrice real insight into her values. Anna may be her motivation but Patrice couldn't bring back the dead.

"I want to meet with her again. I need to find out why hiding is important to understand why she wants people to continue to think she's dead."

"Patrice, have you considered the possibility that continuing to encourage Lidia to return to public life may be inviting unrest?" Clifton was drawn to Patrice's observation the rabble was aching for a leader. Had she considered the symmetry of her situation?

"Since meeting Lidia, I have become aware of the inevitability to which you are referring. While this rising movement is still fragmented, I don't believe waiting any longer to manage their consolidation is in our interests. Had you anticipated a time when the people we serve may want to return to democracy?"

He had, however the knowledge and expertise vested in the Department for almost half a century had the effect of concentrating exceptional individuals. He doubted any consolidation of these outliers would be superior to their current establishment. He was also cognisant Patrice had never had to fight for her power. She did not appreciate the purity of the assent of excellence which had enabled her career to progress smoothly and justly. It had been due to Chen's unflinching rule and determination to ensure an environment where people were safe to excel; and it excluded people whose ability misaligned with their conceit.

"Patrice, are you implying you would like to offer Lidia some form of office in the Department or that you want to give her a political role outside it?"

"Neither. I want to find out what she's planning. I believe without her the others do not have the disciple to collaborate peacefully or productively. They all see themselves as leaders. However, given Lidia's existing profile with ordinary people as an honest and capable political leader who could compete against you, they would almost certainly all fall in behind her."

He hadn't considered Lidia as his rival but it was clever on Patrice's part to transpose and show her through the eyes of those she potentially sought to lead. Patrice was correct. Lidia, if she were to succeed in a challenge, would have to be willing to accept the role of Department Secretary if the current arrangement were to remain. Clifton suspected however she was angling for a return to elected representation not replenishing the current Department Assembly with her followers. He smiled at the prospect of debating her like they had when he was a boy—bright, fiery and emotive.

"Patrice, I appreciate your insights. We have gone far enough down this road alone. This is a fitting time to brief the Department Assembly on your findings before you engage with Lidia again."

"What if she contacts me?"

"Set up a meeting. You can cancel if the strategy changes. Separately, have the Dome gather intelligence on her motivation for staying in hiding."

They attended to other matters and Patrice returned to Department East. Clifton, rarely shaken, felt in light of Patrice's assessment, a reckoning was looming.

21

April sat under a gum tree, beaming and giddy. It was a week she would never forget. Having scraped together her application, April had been accepted into the Accelerated Junior Leadership Program which began with an orientation conference at a winery in the Yarra Valley. Distracted by Lidia and Diamond, she hadn't studied the agenda and arrived sans preconceptions ready to embrace the program.

She was swept off her feet. The venue was breathtaking and the grounds, immaculately landscaped, were endless. They were encouraged to explore the scenery and allow the fresh air to evoke new approaches when stuck on a problem. The conference included presentations from Department Mangers detailing the fusion of good luck and hard work that had propelled them on their respective journeys to the Department Assembly. Guests from diverse backgrounds – sports, arts, business – were invited to share their leadership strategies and provide individual coaching and group mentoring throughout the week, inter-spersed with team challenges and games.

Unlike April's cadetship, which had comprised only maths majors from her year at school, the program was Department-wide and people of all ages and disciplines were invited to participate. A witty engineer caught her eye on the first day and by the last they were inseparable. She sat on the picnic blanket he acquired for them and watched him in the distance talking with his Department Manager about the last seminar of the morning. After the lunch break, they attended the last ses-sion before being dismissed and sent back to their normal jobs. She couldn't believe how fast the week had gone. He worked at Department Central and they arranged to meet after work to study, she was reassured she would be able to see him again before the next program meeting.

As a statistician, leadership had been the farthest thing from April's mind. She had been nervous that Patrice and her Department Manager had been mistaken in their belief she had leadership potential and was relieved to find her curiosity for problem-solving extended beyond data and maths. Reflecting on the week, she was surprised how many of the strategies she used in her work were transferable to solving leadership problems.

Fixated on networking and being noticed by Department Managers, most of the participants were openly and aggres-sively ambitious which she found awkward. She pitied their single-mindedness as they seemed unaware of their beautiful surroundings and expected they were too stressed to enjoy the experience. Hence, she preferred the personal coaching ses-sions. She had been paired with Patrice who was refreshingly calm amidst the hype. They would sneak away and chat about life, their careers and the future. April felt she could tell her anything and was excited they would be having weekly sessions for the remainder of the program. Conveniently, her office was just up the hall.

22

It had played on Clifton's mind in the years before taking Chen's place that the recent past was becoming the distant past. Younger generations, untarnished by the failings of those previous, had benefited from the protection from struggle and were smarter, healthier and happier than older generations. Yet they believed they were immune to the ugliness of the past; they did not appreciate the Department worked tirelessly to maintain the world which enabled them to flourish. They had no awareness of the coordination and demanding work, excellent work such as Patrice was executing, which enabled the world they would inherit. They had no appreciation that their freedom to pursue their interests and excel could devolve back to a world where they had to fight for water and food and housing. However, this was intentional, Chen had designed their governance to unburden them from fear and stress so that they would be able to live their lives in this manner. They were somehow enlightened and ignorant simultaneously.

Clifton enjoyed Department Central at night. Sporadic lights spilled from offices where someone was working late but mainly the building was vacant and peaceful. He walked the promenades, and let his mind churn over problems. Patrice's optimism and blind faith in her ability were a by-product of her success, relative to this manicured world. She had been a cadet in the Department and never left. He didn't underestimate her but she lived in a society where the rules were as real as the machines they were written on. Outside these walls were people who had no regard for her rules and no regard for her reasoning or rational or status here. She was not naive but Clifton was concerned the Department had weakened the resilience of their society to be able to survive adversity. Disbanding democracy was a temporary solution and he had feared their evolution had been stunted when they failed to revert back as originally intended. But was it too late now? Were these people too dependant to be able to enjoy debate and not fear conflict? Patrice was guaranteed to win a fair fight but could she still win when the fight was stacked against her? Was she only savvy here, pitted against other leaders who honourably matched her intellect? These questions had been shifting around in Clifton's mind for long enough. It was time for the Department Assembly to confront for the first time since formation whether their continued governance was in the best interest of the City.

Chen had selected him as her protégé for a reason. On her deathbed she told him it was his task to awaken in their ranks the spirt to fight again. They were sated and it was time to reintroduce competition. Clifton had not grasped at the time what she meant but today he understood what she was doing, giving him her blessing to start a conversation that would end the

Department Assembly. Loyalty to Chen even after her death was absolute. His revelation of her dying wish would be confronting; the seeming antithesis to her legacy. He would need her words to convince his leaders to open their eyes to the possibility there was a better way forward for their City.

23

Absolute chaos was an understatement. Patrice couldn't believe how much disruption eight brats were able to unleash in one night.

She had been woken by her security in the early morning requesting she accompany them to meet Clifton at Department East. This was a code, she was to go to the Dome immediately in line with the protocol for an attack which was significant but did not require the Dome to be locked down. She had not yet been summoned in this way but the City showed no sign of a disturbance so she assumed that, whatever the threat, it had been thwarted. She arrived at the Dome to find a scene which in any other circumstance would have been funny. A group of activists had broken into the City Loop underground train tunnel and constructed a wall at each end of the Department Central Station platform. The Dome was notified of the attack when the first train arrived at the station to find a wall. As it was pulling out of a curve in the track, the train was at reduced speed and was able to stop before it hit the wall. Fortunately, as the activists had cut the tracks in order for them to construct the wall. The damage was going to take days to repair. The station was closed and the Police were confident nothing nefarious had been planted in the building.

Procedurally, this wasn't particularly difficult to resolve. Employees were advised to come back to work the next day but use other methods of transport for the rest of the week due to a technical fault with the signalling. The officers had caught all eight of them, hiding within Department Central, before the workday started. Once in custody, Patrice watched feeds of their interviews. It was clear they knew they would be caught and wanted the Department as a captive audience; each gladly gave a robust account of all the reasons they weren't sorry for their actions and would never stop fighting for their freedom and a return to democracy. Based on their answers, it was unlikely they had any more sinister motives.

The Dome observed the clean up covertly and Patrice spent the afternoon on other matters in her portfolio while crafting the lie she would tell her husband to justify the summons. She hoped he would have heard the train station had been closed and assumed she was involved, negating the need for her to disrespect him yet again.

Before heading home, she spent some time in the apartment preparing a brief for Clifton on the Dome's response to the incident and her assessment of the threat level. Other Department Managers would brief the Department Assembly on their team's performance but she was required to deliver the contextual threat assessment from the Dome as to the impact of the incident on the state of civility.

The incident was not made public. The Chief Operator had not detected any unusual activity before or after and the analysts were satisfied these activists, who were all close friends, were not working with any of their other security priorities. It was clear from their tactics they had no intention of hurting anyone and hadn't been carrying weapons. As a result, they were charged with damage to property and given corrective jobs at the Department so they could be monitored and hopefully rehabilitated. Nevertheless the situation was unsettling.

While crime existed in the City, the Chief Operator had not seen such brazen hostility toward the Department since the Court of Justice was burnt down. The Department was not feared in the community. As a matter of principle, the Department sought merely to provide services to the community. They didn't arbitrarily invade the privacy of their citizens and didn't provide moral or ethical guidance or judgement in the course of their communications. However, the Department Assembly did command authority and utilised their governance structure to showcase and promote excellence. All Department Managers were eminent in their careers and personal lives. All consuming as these roles were, the public and private aspects of their lives were indistinguishable. This culture was highly transparent, and they were all prominent members of their communities.

Patrice secured meetings with several of her trusted advisors within the Department Assembly and found, in spite of the theatrical nature of the juvenile rebellion, many of her colleagues were hurt. She was astonished some of the older members felt these young adults were ungrateful for the carefree and secure world they lived in. It was their overwhelming sentiment that these criminals must have had their minds poisoned against the Department. Patrice reflected on her time with Lidia and suspected that her colleagues' inability to empathise, was not going to illuminate her as to the perpetrators' thinking; or help her protect the City from future threats.

24

After Anna died, Lidia had not expected to feel joy again. The subsequent commitment to their work and avenging her wife was all consuming, gave her purpose, and kept Anna alive in her heart. Yet now reconnected with April, and reflecting on her hilarious afternoon with Patrice, she could feel her resolve waning.

Patrice had sent a request, through Diamond, for Lidia's advice. They met at a secluded beach opposite the Port and sat watching the containers as Patrice told Lidia of the incident in the City Loop. It was Patrice's sad conclusion the subversives must not believe they had anything to live for if they were willing to create a situation which ensured they would be captured. Lidia could hear the concern in her voice, the guilt she felt at their neglect.

They spoke for hours about freedom and the nature of minors and rebellion and concluded it likely the culprits were too young to have registered their own mortality. Patrice received regular updates on their progress and they were reportedly enjoying the work they were asked to undertake which led her to contemplate whether the Department had previously abandoned them. Lidia consoled Patrice and reflected on life before the Department, her life with Anna and their mark on history.

When Lidia initially accepted the invitation, she suspected Patrice wanted to talk about April. Lidia had been regaled of April's transformational leadership conference where she was matched with the most wonderful coach—Patrice. Lidia doubted this was a coincidence and was surprised Patrice would stoop to exploit her position to use a subordinate as leverage. Lidia called her out but was rebuffed. Patrice insisted she had not planned the match, but nonetheless adored her time with April who had spent the whole week smitten with an engineer she was now dating. Interestingly April hadn't mentioned this relationship in Diamond's presence and Patrice was relieved to hear from Lidia that April had also learned something. They agreed Patrice would inform April of her connection with Lidia at their next coaching session. Neither felt comfortable talking about her behind her back.

After learning of the City Loop incident, Lidia consulted with her network. While none knew the offenders, they weren't surprised. Tensions were rising in the suburbs and new clusters of discontent had been springing up. There did not seem to be any recruitment happening, just a natural swelling of the City's youth demanding their potential be acknowledged. Her conversations with Patrice did not indicate the Department was entertaining change but her network collectively felt Lidia was running out of time to emerge on her own terms. The new association between Lidia and the Department had altered her efficacy but, more than that, her relationship with April ate away at her resolve to remain at the Lamasery.

She had also become increasingly conscious of the burden she placed on those whose lives were dedicated to keeping her. When Diamond was young, he relished the secrecy but as he was getting older she was concerned about the impact of his work on his ability to maintain normal relationships—a toll which, in combination with her liaisons with Patrice, was not fair to him or any of her assistants. After prudently deliberating, conscious of the time pressure, she decided to move out of the Lamasery. Diamond took the news well. His job would be the same in the new location but he no longer needed to lie or hide. After the initial shock of her decision, he was more upset April had a boyfriend.

In the long and dark years while Lidia and Anna were separated by her incarceration, they'd planned fastidiously for their future. As a new couple, they had lived in Richmond but had planned once Anna was released to move to the country. Anna, having spent so many years inside a cell, wanted the expanse of the regions and Lidia, having endured her own confinement, found she too wanted to immerse herself in nature.

25

For the first time, Clifton requested the Department Managers assign a full day for the monthly Department Assembly meeting. Over half of them had come to see him to discuss the City Loop incident, fearful of an uprising, and it was time they considered their future. The morning was spent, as usual, with the relevant Department Mangers presenting their findings to the meeting. Clifton asked Patrice to present in the afternoon after he introduced the agenda for the remainder of the day.

The Department was extraordinarily efficient. Decades of rigorous procedures, honest feedback and innovation ensured daily routines were executed flawlessly, the vast experience in their core services enabled excellence. However they were not accountable to the citizens to whom they provided services. Clifton had observed in the younger generations of Department Managers a lack of understanding that, the Governance Rules they implemented were actually a hangover from before formation. A time where the rules were decided by the people in the City and documented in laws. Clifton appreciated it would take months to help orientate the Department Managers who'd never considered their positions contextually; they'd dedicated their lives to serve the City but in reality were imposing their will on its people.

The morning concluded with the consensus that all teams had performed their functions in response to the City Loop incident adequately. The response times were excellent, the containment was effective and the infrastructure had been repaired more quickly than was to be expected given the damage. Yet no one was satisfied; they were completely rattled. They viewed the politically motivated vandalism of precocious rebels like one might a rabid animal with whom one had no hope of reasoning. Their collective cowering was disturbing and Clifton was ashamed at his own leadership; he had not realised the effect of their privileged lives on their ability to see the humanity in all people. They were too sheltered to accept that these people were, from their perspective, fighting for their freedom.

The Department Managers reconvened for the afternoon, eagerly awaiting Clifton's explanation for convening the extended meeting.

"Colleagues. I thank you sincerely for making the time today to be here at the turning point of our existence." A low rumble echoed then dulled.

"Many of you have come to see me in the last weeks, shaken by recent events, to express your concern at this behaviour. Shortly I will invite Patrice to present to you her recommendation, as a result of her investigation following this event, that we increase the threat level."

They gasped in unison. The threat level had not changed since Anna's death. A fact ostensibly too confronting for his most esteemed leaders.

"While Patrice has confirmed without any doubt this was an isolated incident, her investigation uncovered significant disquiet in the community." Another gasp.

"Our citizens are highly educated and intellectual. That they would be itching to express their ideas is not remarkable. What is shocking, is the entitlement in this room." A few had the grace to blush. Others looked outraged at the suggestion they were fallible. He was visibly appalled.

"Most of you did not experience the City before formation but peaceful protest was the cornerstone of freedom. I have been astonished by the lack of curiosity following this incident by all but a select few to seek to understand the actions of our citizens who went to great lengths – and put their lives at risk – to get your attention…"

He was getting louder. Patrice had never seen him yell and hoped he considered her part of the 'select few'. Before meeting Lidia, she would have responded in the same way.

"…and frankly, I am embarrassed that a handful of desperate activists would have you quaking behind your security doors. We have the privilege to do the work we do here because our citizens value our service. Without their support, the authority vested in us to lead no longer exists. These young people were willing to fight to take your power and I ask you this – would you have been willing to fight to keep it?"

Patrice was stunned. She wasn't sure where he was going but she felt the electric current bolt through the room, rousing the sullen autocrats.

"Before Chen died, she told me her life's work to heal her broken City was done and her parting wish was that we return the City to its people. I have questioned whether the City was ready to take control of its destiny and today I stand before you less concerned the people are capable of governing and more concerned you do not have the courage to give it back."

The shame was palpable. A scolding for the ages.

"Now I will leave you in Patrice's capable hands and she will give you a detailed overview of her work and we will meet again after the Department Ball and continue this discussion. In the interim, I implore you to reflect on your role in the governance of this City, consider who you serve, and look back to the history books from before formation and understand how it was our Department Assembly came to be. Your power was never yours to keep, our people let us forget because they were afraid. Let's help to remind them."

He turned his back to the room and strode forcefully to the door and slammed it shut behind him leaving Patrice, lost for words, to pick up the pieces.

26

Diamond was packing the Lamasery for Lidia. She'd purchased and moved to a farm outside Bendigo. She had bought entirely new furniture and appliances. Diamond got the sense she was planning on starting afresh. She had stopped talking about their plans and wanted his help with ordinary assistant work like running errands and mailing letters, which felt strange given he had, until now, delivered every piece of correspondence by hand. He felt like a nice boy helping a sweet old lady, not two people plotting a secret revolution. He couldn't help wondering if he hadn't discovered April in the lane that night whether any of this would have happened. Since they'd met April, both of their lives had changed.

The Department helped Lidia create a backstory and falsify documents so that if anyone looked deep enough they would find she had moved to India after Anna died and recently returned to be with her family. They helped produce some historical articles to understate her absence and set her up with legitimate paperwork and accounts; none of which would have been possible without Patrice, who was apparently Lidia's new best friend.

As he wrapped trinkets and disposed of discarded letters, Diamond conceded he was having trouble walking away from this divine space. Lidia, though he would never admit it, rescued him and kept him out of trouble when everyone else had given up on him. He owed his life to her and had long ago devoted himself to her service. It had not occurred to him that she would ever leave the Lamasery. Especially not alive and apparently ready to move on from her plans, their plans. It was unnerving but she explained part of her reason was she wanted him to have a normal life. He had not even considered any other life. He loved the anonymity and autonomy of the tasks she assigned to him but, since meeting April, he had started daydreaming about what it would be like to be her husband. Then she found someone else and he was forced to confront the emptiness of his lifestyle.

Lidia trusted his judgement. He doubted there was an item in the Lamasery he hadn't seen her use before. She had instructed him to only keep essentials. The last of the other residents had left years ago and she was the only full-time occupant. They decided to remove everything except the furniture but Lidia wasn't sure what she would do with the space. She had asked him whether he would like to move in but it wasn't practical. The lanes were still gated and it was inconvenient getting in and out. In her dreams she would give the Lamasery back to the people when the lanes were reopened. She still wished for the City to experience its tranquillity, but accepted this may not be within her lifetime. After several weeks of removing items indi-vidually, the Lamasery was finally empty and clean and Lidia was reunited with her treasures at her new home.

Lidia had assured Diamond regardless of the change in her location, her plans had not changed. He advised their network, at her request, unless they heard otherwise, to proceed as normal. He was sceptical, having watched the determination gradually drain from her face, but delivered the message nonetheless. Lidia was moving on with her life, April was moving on with her life and Diamond was ready to do the same.

27

Patrice's excuses for the time she was spending at the Dome were becoming more elaborate and her assistants and her husband were becoming wary. Her most recent excuse – that she was learning to play guitar – had been foiled when her husband commented it was amazing her fingers were not callused. Similarly, one assistant discovered she was not at the seminar she claimed to be attending when the falsified speaker came looking for advice at her office. She knew her assistants did not take offence. After years of service to her predecessor and decades at the Department, they would have assumed she had her reasons. Her husband, however, was starting to become tetchy and she too was pained by her deceit, comforted only in the knowledge his appointment to Department Manager was imminent. They anticipated the appointment would be announced at the Department Ball and he would likely be briefed of his portfolio beforehand. She was desperate to be united with him in the challenges the Department Assembly faced.

Rumours there was more to the City Loop malfunction were filtering through the ranks. After Clifton abandoned Patrice during the extended meeting of the Department Assembly, she had spent the reminder of the afternoon trying to de-escalate the pressure by calmly and positively providing the Department Managers with the findings of her investigation. They were irate, in shock, and experiencing the full range of emotions in response to this situation they were unequipped to process. To her relief, they nevertheless trusted Clifton and, as he requested, many spent days in the archives exploring history. Some took leave and went to stay with their grandparents and elderly relatives, the only generation with living memory of the mechanics of that time.

Patrice had become the de facto authority on democracy and entertained a stream of Department Managers, many of whom she had never spoken with personally, now seeking her counsel, looking for a sounding board for the truths their investigations uncovered. She watched as they expanded their reality to absorb alternative futures and slowly accept different outlooks. She felt honoured to be able to provide comfort to her colleagues as they accepted the truth of the past, having recently been through a similar journey herself.

In an attempt to restore her marriage she proposed to take her husband away for the weekend. He was suspicious but accepted. As they were about to leave, he received news he would be appointed to the Justice Portfolio at the Department Ball. She had confessed to Clifton at their last meeting the strain on their marriage and suspected he had intervened to expedite the process when a basket of champagne and treats arrived, wishing them a wonderful weekend away together.

Their distance vanished instantly and the weekend was heavenly. The beaches as they followed the coast were more brilliant than she remembered and she allowed herself to forget the Dome. They talked into the night about starting a family and their roles as future leaders, excited to usher in a new era.

28

April had been invited to the Department Ball and was the envy of Department East. The Ball was legendary. In his decades at the Department, her father had never been and feigned offence that she had received an invitation before him. As a participant of the Accelerated Junior Leadership Program April, along with her boyfriend and the others in the program, was invited to attend the Ball which was held at Government House, the residence of the Department Secretary.

A tradition since formation, the ceremony was dedicated to honouring excellence and celebrating hard-won promotions and victories. She had been told the night would be peppered with intimate and revealing speeches from the Department elite. Patrice would be speaking in celebration of her husband's appointment to the Justice Portfolio. She used April as a sounding board for her speech during their last coaching session and her heartfelt devotion and pride had brought April to tears. She hoped someday to experience such profound love for another person.

April was nervous about wearing a ballgown and Patrice advised her that if she felt apprehensive, she should dress even more formally. Better to be overdressed than underdressed. April had never worn a full-length dress and after a weekend searching, settled on a strapless silk gown. Between styling her hair and make-up and accessorising, by the time she reached Government House she was exhausted.

She arrived early and sat for half an hour watching Department Mangers and their partners arrive. Candidates for Department Manger were groomed from early in their career and consequently many were married to famous people. April supposed this was why tickets to the event were so coveted. She spotted some of her friends and joined them in the queue. The security was stricter than any she had encountered and after a rigorous pat-down by a stern security officer they were allowed inside.

As they proceeded up the drive, the warm glow of the mansion's lights glistened down the path followed by the sound of the band. They entered the foyer, found their seat numbers and were promptly ushered to their tables and served an entrée. She was enamoured by the beauty and majesty of the ballroom. Nearly two centuries old, the walls were lined with monuments memorialising the City and she felt the depth of their history and extraordinary gratitude that she had been invited to experience this significant testament to their shared accomplishments. The high ceiling capturing the echoing laughter above her was more grand than any other building she had visited in the City; she made a mental note to head down to the archives and find out about the architect.

Patrice, one of the last to arrive, floated in on the arm of her husband, her gown billowing behind her. They were a vision and April, who had not seen them together before, immediately noticed her natural glow in his company. Once the ballroom was full, and the first course served, the ceremony began. The speeches, as promised, were good-humoured and grounding. While their individual experiences and the challenges they had faced and overcome differed, they spoke uniformly with affection for one another and exuded competence and grace in the face of adversity.

Once speeches concluded, awards continued in the background as the crowd became restless for formalities to make way for dancing. Patrice came over and introduced her husband to April and her boyfriend and invited them to dinner at Rippon Lea Estate, their first invitation as a couple. Unlike the unbecoming club dancing she had witnessed, skills in ballroom dancing were highly regarded and they had been practicing for weeks beforehand. The guests swayed in time to the roaring brass, April swirled between revolving partners until she was overcome with dizziness and laugher and retired to her table. Watching the dancers attempt to keep time as the guests started to thin, she sat content waiting for her friends to tire, absorbing the fading moments of a spectacular night.

29

After Clifton's imposition, the Department Managers had become disaffected and a rift had formed in the group. The last meeting had produced venom when the contentious democratisation item was revisited. While they, as requested, had undertaken their own reflection, many were unconvinced that change was necessary, would yield better outcomes for the City or was even possible given their current dominance. Childishly, a few challenged Clifton's decision to continue to pursue this matter, demanding they had pressing issues in their portfolios which needed their full attention. Patrice had become Clifton's main confidant and together they spent hours discussing their concerns and ideas. Clifton reminded her it may take years for some of the Department Managers to accept the inherent premise of their leadership; the Formation Agreement was designed to be temporary.

The past weeks had been disconcerting and Patrice was becoming anxious. She reminded her colleagues to be collegial about governance matters during the Department Ball and was assured by the agitators they would disband with grievances for the night. Nonetheless she was on edge.

The ballroom was, as always, glorious. She had been invited several times before and, now a Department Manager, this event would henceforth be the highlight of each year. Delivering the incoming speech for her husband, she was overcome with emotion. Her predecessor had delivered hers and she was privileged to have been asked. On their weekend away they had agreed to start trying to get pregnant and she suspected this was adding to her trepidation. She had stopped drinking pre-emptively and had also altered her diet. Her husband thought this was excessive but she knew she would worry if she didn't so he lovingly vowed to also abstain in solidarity. Not that they drank much anyway; they were too busy.

After her speech and his official appointment he was whisked away, her contemporaries clamouring to impart their wise words inducting him into their ranks. Having experienced this herself, Patrice knew she wouldn't see him for the rest of the night and was feeling overwhelmed. Once the dancing started, she snuck out to take a walk in the Rose Garden to clear her head. Clifton often had roses from the garden in his office and she had questioned whether it could possibly be as splendid as he described. Privately he was quite dramatic.

She walked between the rose bushes surrounded by the floral perfume lingering in the air. Resting on a bench, she admired the landscape design and watched the clouds sweeping past the stars. After a few minutes, she heard people walking around the path. The voices became louder and by the time they reached the end and stopped on the other side of the hedge at her back, she could hear them clearly. Unaware Patrice was sitting on the other side, they continued their private conversation.

"I heard Lidia is alive. A friend of mine saw her at Bendigo Art Gallery. He couldn't believe his eyes. He thought he must have been dreaming and blurted out that he thought she was dead and she laughed and they started talking. It turns out she was living in India this whole time and never remarried. They are going to have tea together next week. I nearly fell off my chair."

Patrice recognised the voices; they were Department Managers. Clifton had – mindful of gossip – decided not to inform the Department Assembly of the Department's covert involvement in Lidia's subtle re-emergence.

"Clifton is talking about bringing back democracy as Lidia mysteriously comes back from the dead. Suspicious timing! Do you believe she was in India?"

"I guess but there have been sightings of her here for years. Regardless, I agree the timing is strange. Even if she's lying, she must be over seventy now, I can't imagine she would be much of a worry to us. I trust Clifton. I've always supported him but he seems to be creating trouble for us for no reason. I don't understand where his preoccupation with democracy has come from. He was loyal to Chen. I doubt she would have wanted him to destroy the Department."

Patrice's blood ran cold. These two were well-reasoned and well-liked. They had not made a fuss like some of the others but they also hadn't voiced these concerns. Perhaps the rift ran deeper than she thought.

"When I committed to the Department I committed for life. I spent a long time thinking about Clifton's outburst. I would be willing to fight to do my work. I love this work and I believe there is no one better than me for this job but I understand what he was saying. I'm not happy he's trying to romanticise the past. Can he not remember how awful those years were before formation? I spoke to some of my older relatives and they can't understand why anyone would want to go back."

"Can you imagine no Department Ball? What a travesty!"

They clinked their champagne glasses together, chuckled and moved on to the latest update on their mischievous grandchildren. Patrice was glued to the spot, afraid to move. They finished their drinks and ambled back to the party. She respected these senior leaders and their dissent was unnerving. They were right. The time before the Department Assembly was awful and many people needlessly died. She wondered if she had been spending too much time with Lidia. In addition to not clearing her head, she found herself considering whether there even was a right or wrong resolution. With the path back to the Ball now clear, Patrice decided tonight the answer didn't matter; she wanted to dance with her esteemed husband. Tomorrow she would tell him about the Dome and then they would work it out together.

30

Lidia's farm had been tenderly transformed into a paradise of animals and plants. The house sat at the end of a long driveway overlooking a gully which wrapped around the back of the property, giving the effect that it was surrounded by a moat. Inside, the building had been recently renovated and the house still smelled of varnish and the gleaming timber boards were hastily becoming scuffed.

While there had been regular visitors to the Lamasery, they had been there to deliver food or provide healthcare or fix broken appliances. Now she was lucky if a day passed without a guest popping in or arriving unannounced with lunch. Having spent so many years alone, her hosting skills were rusty but Lidia quickly readjusted to entertaining. Diamond had spread the word she loved gardening and the verandah which circled the house was filling fast with pot plants. She was flattered so many people wanted to see her settled into her new home.

With Anna in prison, then her decades in the Lamasery, Lidia had only ever known a life which was stationary and was amazed that with every pot plant came news of life moving forward. Patrice visited and, with a wink, refused a glass of wine; Diamond brought a girlfriend he had met at his new job for Lidia's approval which was sweet and unnecessary; April had been promoted and moved in with her boyfriend; and Lidia was reunited with April's father whom, in defiance of physics, had not changed in the slightest. With every visit, the stories of their lives enriched hers and she started to venture into the community. As a result of the backstory the Department devised to explain her absence, people often asked her about her time in India and she had become an expert. After the first few outings, they would find other interests in common. With time, she felt less guilty that all her new relationships began with a lie. She joined a choir and met a group of enthusiastic locals who embraced her as their own and took it upon themselves to show her around the region, now on rotation at her kitchen table. With Diamond only helping her occasionally, and her own schedule full of social activities, all other planning had stalled.

April insisted on throwing Lidia a birthday party at the farm. Lidia, embarrassed by the attention, agreed to a casual barbeque in the afternoon. She was nervous about integrating her lives lest the mistruths not align. By the time everyone arrived, there were dozens of people crawling all over her house. They were showering her in affection and gifts and she was intermittently overwhelmed with love and sorrow and grief and guilt, touched by their efforts to find ever more extravagant and elaborate plants—now a tradition. Upon arrival, guests would immediately inspect any new pot plants, readying to one-up next time they visited. To her relief, as the afternoon progressed, they ceased talking about her and began getting to know each other.

Full and silly, her new friends finally left and Patrice and April stayed to clean up. April, concerned Lidia's cupboards had been left bare, solicited her boyfriend and Patrice's husband to accompany her to the shops to restock. Lidia and Patrice finished the dishes and waited on the verandah for their return. Lidia was grateful for everything Patrice had done for her and recently their professional relationship had morphed into a friendship but the unspoken assumptions they both held were weighing heavily on them. Lidia swayed in the verandah swing, smiling as she rested. So rarely were they alone these days, Patrice knew this was likely the only opportunity she would have to encourage Lidia to divulge whatever she was planning.

"Did your choir friends wear you out?"

Lidia laughed. They were exhausting. "No, I was just looking at the garden. I have been thinking about planting a tree for Anna so she will be with me here."

Lidia's voice was loaded. Even after a day full of people who loved her, she still yearned for Anna.

"That's a nice idea. It's sweet you're thinking of her."

"I'm always thinking of her. She is never far from my heart. Apparently someone from choir has a crush on me. Can you believe it? How ridiculous at this age. I can't even fathom it."

Patrice seized the moment. "You can't fathom moving on from Anna or you can't fathom allowing yourself something to live for?"

Lidia smiled and laughed. "Patrice working me at my own birthday. How tacky!"

"No! Seriously I think you should go for it! But now that you – not me – mention it, I am a bit curious. You chose to move out of the Lamasery without any encouragement from me and I didn't question you at the time but my concerns remain. You were in hiding for some reason and while I don't believe you will ever tell me what you were planning, I would sleep better at night knowing you were retired. And not because of my work—because I care about you." Lidia believed her concern was genuine and sighed at the confrontation.

"Patrice, as always you are compelling. I do believe you care about me. The others will be back any second and this is a conversation for another time. Nevertheless, as you wish, my plans have been such for a long time and they persist without any effort from me," she turned to Patrice, "but you yourself can feel the change coming and that is not my doing."

Patrice was relieved Lidia was open to talking but she was right. Even if Lidia was planning something, she was not responsible for all the volatility which had been bubbling. Clifton had also changed his strategy. She had not told him about the conversation she overheard in the Rose Garden out of respect for her colleagues, but he, nonetheless, had drawn the same conclusion. The subject was still too confronting for the Department Assembly and he had converted to individual meetings with each Department Manager to ensure they had the opportunity to vent their frustrations; guiding them towards enlightened reasoning and away from fear. Patrice could feel the change but doubted Lidia had no involvement.

"Lidia, would you like to meet Clifton? I have gained so much from our conversations and I'm sure he would be interested in seeking your counsel also." Lidia was caught off guard. Another detour in her plans; perhaps it was time to chart a new course.

31

In the distance, April could see hundreds of people covering the steps of Department East spilling out onto the road. As she moved closer she recognised faces of her colleagues who had not been let into the building. She joined the back of the crowd, found some of her friends and learned the doors had not been opened but no one knew why. There had been no explanation and as they waited the mass continued to grow behind them; eventually April was encased by a sea of her peers. They stood patiently, a sporadic shout rang out and eventually officials emerged and announced there had been an incident within the building and they were to go home for the day and come back tomorrow. April, without enough information to be concerned, used the unexpected free time to catch up on her assignment for the Accelerated Junior Leadership Program, one of the only tasks she could do from home.

The next morning, as she approached Department East, she was relieved to see the steps but as she got closer she realised clusters of her colleagues were huddled on the landing between the pillars, consoling one another. Dread enveloped her as she climbed. Security waved her in and as she stepped inside the door she experienced the carnage for herself. She learned from the cleaners that, they had been able to wipe the fake blood off the walls and remove the animal bones from the hallways but had been instructed not to enter the offices. The old Legislative Assembly and Legislative Council chambers had been staged as graveyards to symbolise the death of democracy and the rest of the building had been trashed. She walked towards her office, against the force of her will. The glass in the door had been shattered, the papers ripped from the walls, her work on the boards smudged and illegible and the appliances smashed. She sank into her chair and, as fat sobs landed on her desk, she looked for anything that had survived.

She picked though the piles of slashed papers on the ground and put them in bags, the corners still affixed to the walls. A pointless knock at the door, which no longer provided any privacy, revealed her boyfriend, who'd heard the news upon arriving at his office. He had raced to check on her and stayed for the rest of the day until they'd finished clearing the remains of both her work, and the tapestry which preceded her. Nothing was salvageable. When they left, the office was as empty as the day it was built. She had been instructed to report to Security once finished to advise whether anything had been stolen and was then allowed to go home for the rest of the week while the building was restored.

The investigation discovered the culprits had snuck the blood and bones into the building hidden in a delivery of cleaning supplies and then used the stream which ran under the building to access the old cooling tower in the gardens. They had not been caught and there were no witnesses; no one heard them as there was a concert in the gardens adjacent when the break-in occurred. It was hard to believe the amount of damage that had been able to occur without anyone noticing.

She was grateful she had finished her assignment the night before because she couldn't concentrate. She had nightmares every night and by the time they were able to return to the building she was so exhausted Patrice sent her home. This kind of thing didn't happen here. Her older colleagues said they weren't surprised, they had been expecting something like this to happen after they'd heard rumors of an attack on the City Loop. This time however the perpetrators got away and April was terrified next time someone would get hurt.

32

At the insistence of several Department Managers, Clifton called an emergency meeting of the Department Assembly. After the City Loop incident, they had been stunned and sceptical when he asked them to focus on empathising with the intruders but remained open-minded. Now, in an instant, he saw that progress melt away and the compassion he had started to foster was replaced with unbridled rage. With no suspects or arrests, they focused their anger on Clifton. Due to the nature of the damage, staff were required to be informed about the attack so they could assist with the investigation and many were left traumatised. The damage to the building and the offices was nothing compared to the volume of work they lost. It was estimated they lost between five and ten years of research in the labs which had been completely smashed, the Department Managers directly affected were struggling to quantify how disastrous the setbacks would be into the future.

After it became clear that the people who wanted the meeting were only interested in attacking Clifton, he ended the dialogue and appointed Patrice, together with her husband to prioritise finding the persons responsible; the Department Assembly would reconvene once there was something to report. The Department Manager's fury was intense and justified. There was no point trying to reason with them; they needed time and Clifton had already planned to meet with Lidia.

He had arranged their meeting to take place over dinner in the Rose Garden at Government House. Patrice had mentioned Lidia's love of gardening and he wanted to show off the latest additions to their collection. Lidia was far more vibrant than he expected. They had met once at an award ceremony where Anna was a recipient before formation. He doubted she would recall, but she had barely changed. The force of her personality and her understated elegance were exactly as he remembered.

As etiquette dictated, Lidia was provided with a tour of the buildings and grounds before they reached the Rose Garden. Deferring sitting down to eat, they inspected the bushes and, bold as always, Lidia asked him to arrange for their grounds-keeper to prepare some cuttings for her to cultivate at the farm. She was warm and he appreciated the work Patrice had done to arrange this meeting. Patrice had given them both extensive briefings on the other and as a result they were both relaxed. Their meal was delicious and once the waiters had left them with privacy and dessert Clifton steered them to their agenda.

"It has been such a joy to share your company tonight. I must be honest I am growing weary of the younger generations."

"Likewise, Clifton. Yes. Patrice has commented on the conflicts she's observed. Sounds like she has become somewhat of your confidant?"

He grunted in agreement. "That she has. She is extraordinarily gifted but, to your credit Lidia, I think her time with you and others outside the Department has given her vital perspective as to the nature of power—a virtue I am having difficulty instilling in my other leaders." Patrice had been awakened to another world and Lidia, too, had been impressed at the grace with which she accepted the prejudices of others without judgement.

"You are too kind, Clifton. I certainly have exposed Patrice to standpoints she otherwise would likely not have discovered, but it was her good heartedness which enabled her to befriend an enemy—for that I can't take credit."

"Yes. Once I would have said she would make an excellent Department Secretary but who knows what will become of us all?"

Lidia laughed at the sombre look on his face, slumped in his chair, temporarily captured by his thoughts. "Clifton, don't be so dramatic. Surely things are not so bad for you at the Department? If you are the one stirring for change, these small disruptions must not have you dismayed?"

"I am sulking. I apologise. Thank you for indulging me. You are right I am in the fortunate position to be able to influence the tide and the hard work ahead is not beyond me." Embarrassed, he readjusted himself on the chair. "I appreciate you meeting with me. Do you mind if I seek your counsel on a few matters?"

She nodded. Lidia was amused; even the most powerful man in the City needed an outlet.

"There is a staunch rift in the Department Assembly. I will be vague as to keep our internal matters private but, in the abstract, I wonder whether this is actually derivative of the Department Assembly's partisan origins. You will remember, as many do not, the first Department Managers were a fusion of the government and the shadow government at that time, with some additions thereafter. There is no division ideologically in the Department but, as I mentioned before, I question the inherent nature of power. Perhaps this rift is just illuminating the legacy we are built upon. Our differences had been suffocated by the banality of providing basic services. Now reignited when challenged, I wonder whether the factions are naturally reforming?"

Lidia was blown away. As an outsider she only saw the Department singularly. It was faceless and nameless and that was intentional. Since meeting Patrice, she had insight into the personalities behind the work but had not perceived any dissent to Chen's culture which had flowed seamlessly to Clifton.

"A profound consideration. Not at all impossible but I would look at it another way. Politicians are different to Department Managers. They were accountable to the people who elected them. When presented with a problem, each political party offered different solutions based on their values. While political parties governed, they were supported by departments which had their own apolitical leadership. Perhaps a more practical way for you to look at your predicament is that there are some Department Managers who have the constitution of a politician and some who are excellent implementers?"

He sighed, relieved she had understood; the burden he was carrying dispersed. She was right. He had been trying to invert formation but there were many of his Department Managers who had no aptitude for creativity or policy and were brilliant administrators. Lidia's insights were invaluable; of course many, but not all, would have flair for the rigour of politics.

33

Patrice stopped hurriedly at the nursery on the way to the farm. She was trying to find the giant sunflower in the round pot she'd abandoned last time she visited, in favour of a useful assortment of herbs potted in glazed clay. Her morning sickness was particularly bad and, after the first week of nausea made her late for every meeting, she now added fifteen extra minutes into each item on her schedule. She wasn't sure how much of the queasiness was from the pregnancy and how much was from the stress of the investigation. Patrice and her husband had moved temporarily into the apartment in the Dome so they could use the equipment and be immediately available to the Chief Operator when there were breakthroughs. She was also finding it hard to sleep at Rippon Lea Estate. The threat level had been increased again and while those responsible remained unidentified, she preferred to be at the Dome in case their aggression escalated and she was required for a lockdown.

Leisurely reading in her swing, Lidia smiled broadly when Patrice arrived. They embraced, she dutifully inspected the pot plants and added hers to the row. Lidia had baked Patrice's favourite apricot cookies and they sat on a tray next to a pot of coffee on the verandah.

"I was expecting you would turn up for a debrief. Clifton was delightful. I can see why you enjoy working with him. He is a very quirky man." Patrice's heart sank. She wished she was there to reminisce.

"Unfortunately, I have another reason for being here. Sorry I misled you earlier." She reached into her bag and collected an envelope and handed it to Lidia. Patrice watched as she inspected the contents, waiting for her to realise why she had come.

"I'm so sorry. I'm responsible for the investigation into the attack on Department East so I had access to this evidence before anyone else. I drove up here the second I saw him."

Lidia looked down at images of Diamond crawling out a drain surrounded by people she didn't recognise. She knew what Patrice wasn't saying. She didn't know much about the incident, only that no one had been hurt and invaluable medical research had been destroyed. She was thankful Patrice had told her in person.

"Patrice, I had no idea. No idea! Stupid boy!" Tears of frustration welled in her eyes and brought flashbacks to Anna's death and so many other deaths. She knew Patrice was here as a courtesy; he would be arrested.

"I asked the Department to give me a few hours to see if you could convince him to surrender. His prospects will be infinitely better at the Court of Justice if he comes forward himself. If he gets to us first there may be some leniency. If not, things will be bad for him."

Lidia was furious. He was always overconfident but his temerity was constrained under her guidance. This showy attack did an enormous amount of damage and scared people; she expected more from him but wasn't surprised. He spent his adolescence working alongside her. She supposed it was only natural once he had ceased working for her that he would seek out other activists.

"Thank you, Patrice. I know you will be judged harshly by your peers for delaying his arrest. I will try and reason with him."

Patrice reached out and squeezed her friend's hand, heartbroken by the sorrow which had returned to her face. "If we haven't seen him by nightfall we will go in. He's under surveillance, he can't get into too much more trouble now."

A cry from deep within Lidia escaped before she could stop it and she wept into her hands while Patrice hugged her until she ran out of tears.

"I have to go, they are waiting for me to return. Good luck. I will let you know once we have him." Patrice left her half-drunk coffee, still steaming, on the verandah. Lidia thanked her for the sunflower. She doubted she would be able to look at it without imagining Diamond, wasted and alone, rotting in prison.

34

April was impatient for her next coaching session with Patrice. She was agitated and her strategies to deal with the anxiety which had replaced her normal confident disposition were useless against the never-ending gossip plaguing the Accelerated Junior Leadership Program. Everyone was scrambling to extract truth from the plethora of conjecture regurgitating throughout the group. Rumours about discord between the Department Managers went ballistic. She was exhausted trying to keep up and wanted to see Patrice to confirm whether all or any of the stories were true.

After her office was decimated, she received counselling from the Department; those of her friends not located in the building set about redecorating her office with fun maths posters and pictures of them together. She was touched by their kindness and just as she began to feel better, Diamond was arrested.

She was devastated at the thought her friend targeted a building he knew contained her office. Patrice confirmed through her husband that the Department did not consider the vandalism warranted a death sentence which was a relief. Completely overwhelmed, once the trial date had been set, she tried to console Lidia who was distraught and blamed herself. Consequently, April also felt guilty that they had both abandoned him.

Despite all she had to do to prepare the case against Diamond, while trying to ignore morning sickness, Patrice insisted they not reschedule their coaching session. They met in the Department East gardens under the Federation Oak and ran through their normal agenda checking she was up to date with her program commitments. Patrice relayed April's last assignment had received high praise from the other Department Managers who remarked she possessed insight beyond her years.

However, April was acutely aware she had completed this work before she became stressed and was worried she wouldn't be able to perform to their standards in this state. Patrice listened intently and imparted the wisdom that when you are in a high performing team for a long time, life gets in the way but your colleagues know your capacity and help out while you are dealing with your issue. Then, when you are ready, you go back to your normal workload. She pointed at her stomach as an example and they laughed.

"April, there seems to be more worrying you than these assignments. I know you are scared for Diamond. He will go to prison but he won't be there too long. He needs to be held to account for the damage he caused but he will be safe."

"I'm still angry with him but I'm trying to forgive him. I know he has his reasons. He believes blindly in his cause. Luckily I won't see him for a long time!"

But April was still distant.

"So if it's not work and it's not Diamond what else is on your mind. I don't think I've ever seen you this tense?"

April didn't want Patrice to think less of her by spreading gossip but she desperately wanted to be reassured the rumours weren't true. She let out a defeated sigh.

"I heard some rumours from Department Central that have been causing me to worry about my job. But I don't want to bother you because they probably aren't true."

Patrice resisted an eye roll. "Well, how about you tell me and I promise not to judge you for something someone else said."

She was abashed but accepted the absolution. "It's not that there is one rumour, it's that there are so many. Our group of friends from the Accelerated Junior Leadership Program are based all over the Department and every day there is another wave of rumours. There are a lot of secret meetings of Department Managers. Also, a few people are talking about Clifton losing his touch. Some people have overheard conversations about removing him. Some are talking about quitting. Some have been saying you have too much influence over him." She blushed. "I don't know what to make of any of it. Just that nothing adds up. I don't know if any of it is true and I also don't want people to tell me these secrets!"

April looked worn out by her own misery. Chatter among the Accelerated Junior Leadership Program was nothing new. Patrice also found the inane gossiping tiresome but it was all part of April's education and, if she was to be a Department Manager, April needed to accept interest as a by-product of influence.

"April, I suspect there is some truth in all the things you hear. If you are going to be a leader at the Department you will be surrounded by gossip all the time but most of the rumours are just part of being one person in a team with lots of moving parts. Everyone is just trying to find their place and do what they think is in the best interest of the City."

April considered this; it wasn't the denial she was looking for but she was relieved to have off-loaded her concerns. Patrice gave her a hug and sent her back to the office. Patrice stayed to rest and think under the tree. Looking up at the Dome, she wondered whether they too had heard her colleagues plotting Clifton's demise.

35

April's boyfriend was away on a study tour and, missing him too much to sit in their apartment alone, she went to visit Lidia at the farm. Welcoming the company, Lidia planned a weekend of adventures and baking. Relishing the escape, thoroughly fed up with the Department, April defiantly stayed for a whole week. In an act of rebellion, Lidia had arranged all the pot plants by size and required her visitors to reorder them every time they added to her collection. April reasoned, if Patrice was grooming her to be a leader, she would have the rest of her life to be suffocated and decided to enjoy the outdoors and Lidia's wicked sense of humour while she still could.

Once April had disbanded all her responsibilities back home, Lidia suggested they spend the week building a shed. Trinkets were piling up and Lidia thought it seemed like something April's maths brain could figure out. April, aware that with

Diamond's sentencing coming up Lidia needed a distraction, agreed supportively to the project.

The mission of two people who had never built anything before evolved into a community endeavour. Lidia's new friends dropped in with tools and wood and paint until eventually, shockingly, a shed with a roof and double doors stood shining at the end of the garden—a victory they both needed. Lidia invited all the contributors back for a completion party to celebrate what had been the most elaborate construction of a shed in anyone's memory.

April didn't want to go back to the City. They'd had so much fun and she couldn't remember ever spending time with people so uninhibited. Lidia didn't feel like an aunt. She was mischievous and playful and April felt sad when she focused on the years they had lost.

Since Lidia had moved to the farm it felt like she had always been there. When she lived at the Lamasery, Lidia had tried several times to talk to April about her plans but had ceased recalling the past. While she had many new friends, Diamond had been taking care of her for years and yet Lidia seemed unaffected by his sudden departure. April wasn't sure how to ask if she would be alright without him and not sound condescending but nevertheless she was worried about Lidia here alone without anyone to help her. They sat down for their final dinner together before April's boyfriend returned home from his trip. Lidia hadn't mentioned Diamond at all in the last week and April didn't want to leave without trying.

"So, how are you coping without Diamond? Have you been able to find someone to replace him?"

"I was hoping to forget about him." Not the response April was looking for.

"No, I mean he used to help do things for you around the house. Do you have someone to help you here now he's gone?"

She frowned. "He didn't help me around the house. He assisted me with communications and logistics from the Lamasery, things I can do for myself now I can leave the house!"

Lidia opened the door and before she could shut it, April pounced. "So does that mean you don't need to communicate in secret anymore? You have stopped whatever you were doing then?"

Lidia hesitated while thinking of a delicate answer.

April's voice became squeaky. "Lidia I am your niece. I have a right to know! You have such a wonderful life now. I don't want to lose you like we lost Diamond." She broke into tears.

Patrice had warned Lidia that April was nursing a short fuse. April had resolutely refused to acknowledge Lidia's plans, and Lidia assumed April still wasn't interested, but, in light of Patrice's forewarning, she should have been more careful. Lidia moved to the other side of the table and put her arm around April and tried to reassure her.

"April, I'm not going to prison. I haven't committed any crimes. My plans have been in place for a very long time and soon all of my work will become apparent. You don't need to worry about me. I spent years burying people I love. I have no appetite for mayhem. I would never leave you unless I had to and I would never put you or your father at risk."

April paused crying. "Why all the secrecy before then if what you're doing isn't really that bad? Why did you leave us if you didn't have to!" Tears returned.

"I left to keep you safe. The Department was hypersensitive for years after the Anniversary Attacks and once Anna died, they would have acted first and asked questions later. It wasn't a risk I was willing to take. We all made sacrifices. Anna paid with her life, as did many others. I know you resent the years we lost but just think, if you hadn't come looking for me in that lane, we may never have met. I would have gone to my grave alone to protect you and I still would."

April believed her but was too overwhelmed to continue arguing and was content Lidia would be able to manage both her house, and her mysterious affairs, without Diamond. They spent the rest of the evening marvelling at the shed and planning a gift for Patrice's baby.

April said goodnight, leaving Lidia writing letters on the kitchen table, when she halted abruptly, reminded of a question which had been slipping her mind.

"Lidia, do you remember I told you at the bar I found out about the lanes in a love letter to my father from someone living at the Lamasery? Do you know who it was? I was never brave enough to confess I had broken into the filing cabinet."

She grinned. "It was me. The letters were an anagram between your father and I. The decryption key would have been on the envelope – three words under a shield with a clock and a bird."

April laughed and said goodnight, relieved she wouldn't have to unravel another mystery.

36

Patrice was becoming concerned the excitement of a 'Dome Baby' was distracting the staff. While the Chief Operator had indulged excessive preparations for a birth in the building's barely touched surgery, his tacticians knitting at their consoles tested his patience. Nevertheless, having her baby at the Dome was the most practical solution. Clifton agreed while Patrice and her husband were living at the Dome as new parents they could share the responsibility for oversight of its operations, which was a relief for both of them.

Once Diamond's accomplices had been arrested, the threat level was reduced and Patrice was free to spend more time with the off-duty staff; who were busily searching for the illusive connection between the subjects they were surveilling that they believed to be evading them.

After meeting with April, Patrice consulted the Chief Operator as to the extent of their surveillance of Department

Managers. He was clearly uncomfortable, sensing an impending request but obliged. He explained the Dome was required to vet all potential candidates for Department Manager prior to appointment however, as most had been groomed for the roles from early in their careers, there was very little which concerned the Chief Operator. She understood, Patrice and her husband had been provided with personal security for years and were used to the intrusion. In the course of their monitoring, the Dome's analysts regularly intersected with Department communications and were sometimes troubled by the confessions they intruded upon but generally the fantasies of Department Managers for power or glory were not a concern to the Dome.

Patrice was intrigued. Aware of the ethical boundary she was nudging, she presented her awareness of rumblings of a coup within the Department Assembly; he was touched by her naivety. He explained that at any one time many Department Managers were forging their own path and – as always – they were aware of the current heightened discord but he assured her that those testing the waters now, had been planning for this day for a long time. He concluded that concerns of the Dome related to threats to the City. A change in Department Secretary, however uncouth, was outside their purview.

Patrice, while grateful for his honest counsel, felt the weight of the unknown return. His explanation reminded her of the person she knew who had obfuscated detection for decades. Lidia had been so bold as to advise Patrice her plans were still in place. Expanding her mind and disbanding her affection for her friend, she could no longer ignore the nagging sense Lidia was somehow involved in the current dissonance. Mindful of her enormity, once the baby arrived it would likely be months until she could get to the farm. Lidia had evaded her long enough. Time had come for Patrice to force the point.

37

After his illuminating dinner with Lidia, Clifton created a list with the Department Managers he thought would be good politicians in one column, and those which he thought were naturally suited to management in the other. Once Patrice had instigated the peaceful surrender of the crew who'd vandalised Department East, the Department Managers had begun to defuse and his individual sessions recommenced. Approaching each of them with different strategies based on his new classifications had garnered excellent results and he wished he'd had the idea himself. With each rotation, their concerns evolved and he believed they had come out of a phase he called 'acceptance' and had entered a phase called 'it will never work'. A third of the way through the current round he realised they wouldn't be able to move forward if he couldn't answer their fundamental practical questions about how democracy used to function.

The Court of Justice was appointed by the Department Assembly and Clifton had excellent relationships with the leadership. After formation the Governance Rules were approved by the Development Assembly and the Judges, over time, disbanded with statutory interpretation and started inviting Department Managers to participate in adjudication. This collaborative approach was not particularly controversial because the Governance Rules where never meant to replace the undisputable authority of written statutes made in the Parliament. As a result it was quite normal for Judges and Department Managers to meet and work through issues together.

Clifton had been snooping in the Court of Justice archives trying to find the answers he sought. Eventually, word that he wouldn't let anyone help him had spread to the Chief Justice who came down to the basement and hauled him up to her office, demanding to know what he was doing. He explained he was trying to figure out what the laws were when the Formation Agreement came into effect and whether they would still be current if they reverted back to a parliamentary democracy. He emphasised he was only curious and it was vital no one know what he was looking into lest they read meaning into his actions. She was unconvinced but agreed to prepare the advice herself – alone – and get back to him.

The Department Assembly was meant to govern using the Governance Rules for twenty years while the laws were paused to be revived at the expiry of the Formation Agreement. As a result of the permanent installation of the Department Assembly the laws as they previously existed were, in effect, permanently suspended in time. There was no concern when the Formation Agreement was drafted that there was anything wrong with the laws; it was the customs and norms of society which had eroded.

It took some time to review all the laws and compare them with the Governance Rules but the Chief Justice found most to still be relevant. She advised Clifton that, by adhering to the Parliament's rules, assuming the hypothetical parliamentarians understood how to make law, politicians could easily update the laws to accommodate the changes which had occurred in the last five decades. She caught the glimmer in his eye. She doubted a Department Secretary would be rummaging in their basement unless they were planning something. She was glad, she had been expecting this request a decade ago.

38

Lidia opened the door, unexpectedly finding Patrice on the verandah clutching two suitcases and a bunch of flowers.

"Hello, I've come for your plans and I'm not leaving until you tell me everything...." She dropped the bags, "... and I couldn't lift a pot but here are some flowers." She thrust daffodils at Lidia and lurched herself into the swing. "I'm serious I'll have this baby right here on the verandah if I have to!"

Lidia laughed, she had no doubt whatsoever Patrice would stubbornly have a baby on her verandah. "Hello. Thanks for the flowers. Looks like you've got me right where you want me. Too bad you aren't going to be able to get out of the swing without my help." They dissolved into laugher. "What's in the suitcases? Are you planning on torturing me or do you think it will take you months to break me so you brought every piece of clothing you own?"

Laughing even harder now, they couldn't speak. Poor Patrice. Something had obviously happened to provoke this outrageous stunt. Once she caught her breath, Lidia gave in. "Oh Patrice. I refuse to let you in the house. You are going back to your husband. Wait here, I will make you some tea and give you the short version. I have some cake left over from choir."

Patrice, relieved she could go home, sat patiently wondering whether there were any other ways she could exploit this pregnancy which was proving a potent elixir. Lidia returned with the tea and caramel mud cake and settled on the wicker lounge.

"I'm not sure where to start. Your use of the word plan implies there is an end goal but that was never really how we were set up."

"Who is we?"

"This is going to take a very long time if you keep interrupting me."

Patrice mimed locking her lips and throwing away the key.

"A better way to describe where we are now is to understand what we were trying to achieve. You would be too young to remember Anna dying. In the last years of her sentence, there was renewed optimism a return to democracy would be possible and the anticipation of her release generated its own momentum. People started to mobilise naturally around her without her involvement, she inspired an entire generation. While her death was barbaric, separately to my grief, I understand why they killed her. The Department Assembly was reacting desperately to a situation it didn't know how to control, its calculation was accurate. Without the synergy her inspiration created those who sought to follow her lost their orientation. When they killed her they were really killing hope. It wasn't about Anna."

Patrice was mesmerised by the sadness and compassion in her voice.

"After the Court of Justice was burnt down many leaders reached out to me. They questioned whether the effectiveness of killing Anna at thwarting the movement, was an indication their resolve to return to democracy was actually being driven by retribution for the executions following the Anniversary Attacks. We all agreed if there was to be any hope at a return to democracy it could not rely on one person. It must be born of the desire to self-govern not the desire for revenge. As a result, we decided to build our own political network so when the time came organically, which we all believed it would, we would be ready to lead."

Patrice was blown away. How could a political network exist within the City and the Department not know about it? Surely the Dome would have been aware if such a web existed. Perhaps Lidia was overstating her influence.

"What do you mean by a political network?" Lidia, sensing Patrice's frustration, reminded her not to interrupt.

"I know you want me to tell you the facts of what and where we are but I expect you will pick up your bags and run back to the City. It is important you understand the context. You are trained to detect and remove threats. The nuance of governance was lost and in exchange for the facts you must listen first to the history."

Patrice was getting hungry and suspected her impatience needed fuel. She suggested they break for lunch. Lidia fixed her some pea soup and Patrice ate while she continued.

"I appreciate hearing there is a network of which you are unaware is confronting but, while we believe in democracy, we remember – I remember – the desolation which necessitated the Department Assembly. People were so poor that couples stopped having children for fear they wouldn't be able to feed them. Homelessness was rampant and, amidst the chaos, maintaining the discipline needed to plan and construct infrastructure and buildings was impossible. The obligation on the rich to uplift the poor which had underpinned the success of democracy had been eroded and greed bred more greed until the tenants of civility were disbanded. Trust, taken for granted, was left to wilt and died while people scrambled to survive."

Lidia felt ashamed of that time, as did everyone who lived through it. The frenzy of fear and the speed with which people turned on each other revealed dark capabilities of which no one would have previously thought themselves able.

"Chen saved us. Without her intervention to form the Department Assembly, all civility would have been lost. The force with which she commanded what was left of the political class restored order as quickly as it had devolved. Once her plan to return our dignity was in place we began to crawl back to our former respectability."

Patrice was confused.

"There is no one who doubts Chen saved this City. But it was not democracy that caused the breakdown of our society. It was the people. Without democracy, without the freedom to live and create, there would have been no City to lose. For a brief moment in time, our leaders led us to believe all we needed to succeed was our own ambition and soon the duty to one another inherent in our shared existence was forgotten. We lost our freedom because we did not appreciate the effort required to maintain it. Chen understood this and forced the abandonment of aspiration while we relearned the obligations of human society."

Patrice understood what Lidia was trying to say. "I'm sorry you had to go through that. You were very young then, you're not responsible for the failures of the generations before you."

"No, but nonetheless the Department has had the same effect. Instead of temporarily releasing us from the pressures of self-determination in order for us to rebuild society, the Department took over so pervasively it negated the need for trust. The trust between strangers which allowed for exploration and innovation and creativity was lost but it was never rebuilt, just moderated."

It hadn't occurred to Patrice before now that Lidia, whom she adored, may be about to divulge information she would be forced to report to the Chief Operator.

"I appreciate where you are coming from but I fail to under-stand how this relates to your plans now. Lidia, are you able to be honest without implicating yourself in a crime?"

She laughed. She doubted Patrice would be able to find any evidence of her involvement even if she wanted to arrest her but reassured her she would be vague.

"It was evident to us, that when the societal wounds healed sufficiently to enable the Department Assembly to consider returning the Parliament, it would take time for political organisations to re-establish. It was our goal to use the time in-between to build a political network with its sole purpose to rebuild trust in community. We used the old electoral maps and appointed custodians of each segment. Over time, those custodians have grown their own local networks but they don't coordinate with anyone but me. It has never been our intention to agitate for democracy or even actively pursue democracy, only to keep it alive."

Patrice was satisfied she knew just enough. "Thank you, Lidia. I'm relieved to hear your plans are, on the surface, benign but there is still potential for disaster in the wrong hands."

"Yes, of course. Look at the recent behaviour we have seen. Youth impatient for its freedom. You would be astonished at how many similar plots our custodians have foiled over the years."

"And here I was thinking we were doing such a good job!"

They laughed, the tension between them gone. Patrice was grateful for the time to get to know Lidia before they had to have this conversation. The revelation, if they had not built the trust they now shared, would have been terrifying, as if to attest Lidia's thesis on community.

Lidia had once said the rift they were experiencing at the Department was not her doing but Patrice was not so confident. "Do you have people in the Department?"

Lidia took a moment to choose her words carefully. "Your question implies obligation, people who have come to share and promote democratic values are not as a consequence expected to pledge any sort of allegiance. Nevertheless, I understand what you are asking and the answer is no. We felt it would be a waste of resources."

Patrice knew exactly what she was saying. They had taken the Local Councils. She didn't want to hear anymore; she'd learnt enough. She relaxed into the swing.

"No more, Lidia, or you will shock me into labour!"

39

Clifton stood, resolutely and defiantly at the head of the Department Assembly, next to a box of prized mementos and vases, fed up with their astounded faces.

"I announce today with immediate and permanent effect my resignation from the employment of the Department and the esteemed position of Department Secretary. I have arranged for Patrice to act in the role of Interim Department Secretary until such a time you can arrange yourselves to appoint a new leader." They stared at him in stunned slience.

He reached into the box and pulled out a stack of envelopes and proceeded to walk around the room, handing each a letter.

"In these envelopes is advice from the Chief Justice outlining, in the legal opinion of the Court of Justice, the steps required to reinstate the Parliament."

They each read the single page and looked at each other confounded.

"Your forebears designed the Formation Agreement which established this Department Assembly with an end date, after which all laws which were previously in effect before formation would be reactivated. The Department Assembly exists because the end date was removed. I am assured by the Court that all you need to do to dissolve the Department Assembly is amend the Formation Agreement by a simple majority vote and reinsert an end date." He looked around the room and made a mental note of which Department Managers were smiling.

"As I walk out of here today, I intend to build a new political party and when I have done that I will come back for my job the honourable way, with the blessing of the people. I believe in the people and I will spend the rest of my days proving to them how much more we can achieve when we are all involved in the governance of this marvellous City."

Patrice and her new daughter were at the Dome waiting for news his resignation had gone smoothly. He picked up his box, slammed his fist on the table, then walked out the door.

40

April and her boyfriend fit together perfectly and she woke every morning amazed she loved him more than the day before. They'd finished the Accelerated Junior Leadership Program which was a huge relief and their reclaimed free time brought them even closer. She'd never seriously dated anyone but from the second they met, she knew there would be no one else. Living together was more enjoyable that she could have imaged; his time away only reinforced how life with him transformed every day into an adventure. They never fought. They enjoyed the same activities and kept the same punishing hours. She was deliriously happy. Given how challenging things had been outside their relationship for both of them, she was caught completely off guard when he asked her to marry him. Regardless of his declaration of love at first sight – the antithesis of his rational engineering mind – she believed he truly knew her and would love her eternally.

Upon arriving back at Department East after the proposal, she was pleased Clifton had stolen her thunder by walking out of the Department Assembly. The ensuing pandemonium let them savour their private moment away from prying eyes. Patrice was an excellent replacement for Department Secretary. While she was younger than most of the other Department Managers, Patrice was exceptionally well-regarded and they felt she was most equipped at navigating the challenges which lay ahead. April liked Clifton and wondered what could possibly have driven him to storm out but today she didn't care about the Department; there would inevitably be an explanation, or failing that a rumour.

Diamond had been sentenced to five years in prison. The intruders hadn't realised the value of the research they had destroyed which correspondingly increased the punishment required for justice to be realised. The sentencing Judge was harsher than anyone expected, given their non-violent actions, commenting 'If you don't know what you're smashing, you shouldn't be smashing it'.

April went to support him at the hearing on the days he was allowed out of prison to attend. He looked drained but not too skinny which was more than she was expecting. It was awful to see him there but he had a positive attitude and planned to study as part of his rehabilitation. He was excited and looking forward to the future and April was reassured he wasn't as depressed as either Lidia or his girlfriend who were both perpetually in tears. In contrast, he told her when she went to visit him that he had achieved nothing in the past five years so if he could walk out of prison with a qualification it would be five years well spent.

After lunch at the dining hall she left early and sat on the bench outside her office window and contemplated the richness of her life now compared to before she found Lidia. In such a short time she had experienced extraordinary highs which challenged her capacity for love and compassion but also pain, disappointment and exhaustion. Lidia had never pressured her or imposed her values but the possibilities, variety of people and breadth of opinions available to her now, without question, dwarfed her previous life. She felt refreshed and joyful, unphased by the chaos unfolding around her. Looking down at the ring sparking on her left hand, she marvelled at how much had changed.

41

Lidia sat with her back pressed against the architrave and admired the skyscape. In the comparatively short time since she'd been away from the Lamasery, the City hadn't changed. She thought it might have moved on without her. The last few days had been hectic and she felt small in its familiar expanse. She sipped ginger tea as Clifton padded about the barren spaces arranging his few possessions. As Diamond had managed the packing after she'd moved to the farm, she hadn't seen the space empty. She was in awe of its raw beauty. So many years had passed since they'd first sought refuge in its safety, she'd become desensitised to the Lamasery's majesty.

Clifton was excessively energised but she didn't know him well enough to be certain whether she should be worried. It turned out he had not correlated he would not be able to go back to his residence in Government House and was now homeless. The staff didn't actually know he'd resigned until someone from the Department arrived to discuss the arrangements for his departure. As he had lived in Department properties most of his life, he didn't have a residence in the City.

Patrice generously invited him to stay at Rippon Lea Estate, as they were still at the Dome, while he found somewhere to live. After she issued the offer, the Chief Operator warned her Clifton was now at the top of their current priorities list and, while he wasn't even slightly concerned Clifton would do anything to hurt the City, they would prefer to avoid the Department Secretary harbouring security threats. Patrice, goodhumoredly in her exhaustion from nursing, asked Lidia whether the Lamasery was still empty and Lidia had kindly relocated him by the end of the day.

Lidia needed to get back to the farm to tend to the animals and had brought enough food for him for a few days while he came to terms with his new abode. He was winding down and she invited him to join her in the window for tea. Lidia watched him cautiously. She wanted to make sure he was alright before she left. He seemed to have made the most important decision of his life on a whim. He finished unpacking and joined her on the seat.

"Clifton I am a little nervous to leave you…" He looked puzzled, and she added, "…because you quit your job with nowhere to live?"

"Ah yes. Not to worry. Where I rest my head of an evening is of no consequence to me. As you can see, I have very few belongings. We…." He corrected himself, "They, at the Department, are used to being shuffled around. I am quite used to not having a home."

A persuasive excuse but she wasn't convinced. "Nevertheless Clifton, I only want to be assured you're alright before I leave.

You made a very significant decision and, regardless of whether you felt attached to your home, you didn't arrange anywhere to live which makes me think you couldn't have been planning to resign very long?"

"Lidia, I'm not just alright, I'm great!" He jumped off the sill and danced on the spot. Then, registering the alarm on her face, realised this was not helping ease her concerns and sat back down. "Forgive me, Lidia, I feel like I just woke up for the first time. I haven't had a chance to talk to Patrice or anyone really about the revelations of the past few weeks." He held up his hand to pause the conversation and went to retrieve one of the leftover letters in the box from his office. She was wary.

"The City Loop incident forced me to confront the tension which, as we have previously discussed, had been gradually building for some time. I initially resisted the transition but once I accepted sentiments were changing, in spite of us, I tried to lead my Department Managers so that they too would accept the change."

He handed her the envelope and she read the brief advice from the Chief Justice, absorbing its concurrent complexity and simplicity.

"In a confluence of practicality, morality and obligation I understood what is able to be done simply will not be done without the burden of responsibility being completely absolved. The question I was seeking to answer was, what gives the Department Assembly the authority to govern the City? The Formation Agreement established the Department Assembly and gave it authority to establish Governance Rules to govern the City. But the actual Formation Agreement document, was essentially, legally, a contract.

Lidia looked baffled, he tried a different approach. "Essentially the Department Assembly was formed by a contract between all the people who had power in the City at that time who agreed to the terms of the contract. Which is why the Department Assembly was able to continue governing so easily by removing the end date in the contract rendering it valid in perpetuity. Inversely, the Department Assembly can be similarly dissolved by inserting an end date into the Formation Agreement and waiting for that date to pass. The Formation Agreement can only be changed by the Department Assembly. We need to convince the Department Assembly to end itself."

She nodded. He needed to force them from the outside because he couldn't do it from the inside.

"I understand what you're saying but that doesn't explain the rash decision-making on your part. What was the urgency?"

He acknowledged her apprehension. "Yes, perhaps I didn't have to quit that second…" He looked sheepish, "…but as I said, everything aligned. Patrice told me about your network and, while I admit I know nothing about it, as soon as I got this advice from the Chief Justice I knew exactly what I needed to do and exactly how we have to get there."

She still wasn't convinced he should be alone, but was relieved he was at least aware his behaviour was impetuous.

"I have been tinkering around the edges for months but now with the support of enough people and the right pressure at the right time – with a lot of warning and no violence – we may be able to get the traction we need to force the decision into the hands of the people. Lidia, I honestly don't think, given the sensitivity of the past, anyone else will be able to do this. It must be subtle and flawless. I may not succeed but I must try. For Chen, for the City, for myself."

She looked into his earnest eyes and held his stare. It was time. Finally.

42

Upon receiving news of her appointment as Department Secretary, the family was relocated from the Dome to Government House. By accident, Patrice discovered the antidote to her daughter's restlessness was to walk around the ballroom and introduce her to the paintings and statues which lined the walls. There was much debate among the staff as to the reason—some believed she was destined to be a historian or an artist, others believed it was because she loved meeting new people. Patrice thought it was probably the shiny picture frames. Nevertheless, whenever Patrice proclaimed she was headed to the ballroom, they knew not to bother her.

Patrice was surprised at how quickly her colleagues had appointed her to the position permanently. She suspected they were unnerved by the pace at which views were changing and believed Patrice would be able to wrangle Clifton. It was bittersweet. Patrice had, with great sadness, ended her friendship with Lidia as her involvement with Clifton created a conflict she couldn't reconcile. Lidia knew enough about the Department to know Patrice would not hesitate to intervene against her at any inclination of potential unrest. Patrice knew them both well enough to know they would be planning something but trusted it would not be violent and cast them from her thoughts, she needed to focus on preparing the Department Managers to be ready to defend themselves in an intellectual battle.

In the aftermath of Clifton's dramatic exit, her husband – in his capacity in the Justice Portfolio together with the Court of Justice – prepared a brief for the Department Assembly on their options. Having reviewed the advice, Patrice invited the Chief Justice for dinner and their legal discussion quickly became philosophical.

The Court was asked to give a legal opinion as to the origin of the authority of the Department, and the legitimacy of the Formation Agreement giving the Department Assembly the authority to create and maintain the Governance Rules. In essence, it was the Chief Justice's view that the Formation Agreement was originally entered into and agreed upon by people who had been elected to make decisions on behalf of the citizens in their capacity as their representatives. The legitimacy of the Department still flowed from the foundational assumption that the Department Assembly was the form of government the people had chosen. There were no rules preventing anyone from challenging that assertion. Without being tested, there was no evidence to show that governance by the Department Assembly was not the will of the people. Unless there was some form of uprising, governance by the Department Assembly was either an expression of its genuine authority, as the people's preferred form of government, or the people were oppressed; and there had been no recent evidence to prove or disprove either thesis.

Patrice tried to comprehend the extraordinary coexistence of consent and oppression illuminated by the Chief Justice and was impressed by her ability to articulate so profoundly their conundrum. As she left, thanking Patrice for dinner, the Chief Justice said sympathetically, 'The only way you will know your authority is legitimate is if someone tries to take it from you'.

Long after her daughter fell asleep, Patrice continued to pace the floor of the ballroom searching the memorials of her forebears on the walls for a peaceful resolution to this insoluble predicament.

43

Clifton's progress was being stunted by his need to shop for food, cook, eat, clean and wash his own clothes. Always grateful for the assistance provided by the Department, he'd not appreciated how much of his productivity could be attributed to his kept state. Fortunately, any time spent within the Lamasery doing chores was also contemplative and he felt sad that its beauty was trapped within the lanes gated away from the people it was built to console.

Since taking residence at the Lamasery, his initial clarity never faltered and the planning was proceeding at an acceptable rate, given the Department's efforts to hamper his campaign. As he had the benefit of being able to educate the Department Managers before he left, there was now a growing number of supporters on the inside defending his actions. Having literally written the rule book, he knew how to argue his way out of the obstructions they were creating. He was grateful they were trying to defeat him legitimately. With anyone other than Patrice as Department Secretary he would have expected to have been found in a gutter well before now. Regardless of their opinions, all the Department Managers acknowledged the validity of his arguments and support for him in the community and resolved privately – as long as he was not planning anything violent – they would have to fight him in daylight.

Lidia was proving to be an excellent sounding board and had reluctantly agreed to be the face of the campaign. His plan relied heavily on the network she had built and eventually, after demonstrating all the safeguards he would put in place to ensure their safety, she agreed to work with him.

His plan centred upon the end date being reinstated in the Formation Agreement and they agreed the fifty year anniversary was an auspicious date on which to campaign for the end of the Department Assembly. They also hoped this would focus the energy of any overzealous outliers and prevent any misguided heroics. After much debate, they settled on the slogan 'End Date, Election Date' which gained traction with Lidia's choir who were bribed with cheese and wine to provide feedback on the shortlist. Catchy and brief, it won the vote unanimously because they felt it was clear about what the campaign wanted to achieve. They had come as far as they could in the planning stage and it was time for action.

It had taken a long time to convince Lidia to involve the custodians—almost as long as it had taken to convince her to reveal the extent of her network. The custodians had been chosen after Anna died and while some of the original appointments were still in place, most had passed on the responsibility to their successors. Some had died and a few had been cut off after being careless with Lidia's security. Clifton had been mortified on behalf of the Department at the comprehensiveness of her influence.

They had one custodian in each area who communicated with Lidia. That person had between two and four potential successors and they had countless numbers of people who considered themselves to be a team, although she was very strict about keeping the boundaries vague; they understood the expectation that they not identify as a group or seek to name or define their association. The only ritual which united them was the induction session the successors were required to undertake to ensure Lidia's protection.

As soon as Lidia amassed a handful of future custodians, they were invited to the Lamasery basement where Diamond gave them training. The successors were all provided with emergency channels should something happen to their custodian. They were taught how to use the anagrams and he gave them a brief overview of the coordinating role Lidia played and reinforced the importance of the fluidity of their shared interest. Lest anyone be caught, their connections would remain invisible.

From her window in the Lamasery, there had been a direct line of sight to several rooftops below where messages could be left for her by arranging equipment in certain patterns. Some rooftops held letter boxes for urgent correspondence which could not wait until Diamond was available to collect the message in person.

Once she relocated, the custodians continued corresponding by writing letters to her at the farm, however maintaining the anagram. With the Department now in her life, maintaining any pretence was futile. Many of the custodians had visited her at the farm but still did not have any knowledge of each other.

Lidia wanted assurances from Clifton, before she involved the custodians, that they would not be arrested. Lidia wanted him to guarantee they would be allowed to challenge the authority of the Department Assembly without any repercussions. Clifton had become stuck. It was clear to him that the only path to forcing the Department to acknowledge the will of the people to self-govern was to show it tangible proof of dissent which evidenced their continued governance was illegitimate. He pained over a strategy to also keep them safe.

Clifton sought an audience with the Chief Justice who refused to meet him. He turned up at her house and managed to charm his way in. It was her opinion it was not illegal to protest nor was it legal to protest. The Governance Rules were not designed with dissent in mind given their singular nature but it was her view that, because the CBD was gated, regardless of the legitimacy of protest, entering without a permit was still illegal. She clarified that groups of people could, hypothetically, gather outside the CBD and it would not be illegal; nonetheless she doubted he would be able to organise an event of any meaningful scale without being intercepted. Flinching at the twinkle in his eye, she tenderly told him to leave before he got them both in trouble.

44

Lidia opened the door to find Clifton arms outstretched with a square tiled pot overflowing with rosemary. She had been hoping for someone less demanding.

"I am so sick of you."

He was undeterred. "Human chain!"

She smiled waiting for an explanation.

"Human chain!"

"Why do people keep turning up at my farm without an invitation! Do you think if you keep saying 'human chain' at me I am somehow going to know what you mean?"

She passed him, collecting the pot. Amused at his excitement, she sat in her swing. Evidently he was not leaving.

"I have a guest arriving for lunch shortly. You aren't invited. You have ten minutes."

"That's all I need." He rubbed his hands together. He had clearly prepared a pitch on the way up and she was hoping this would be quick.

"We need to protest. I know you don't want to ask people you care about to expose themselves or your networks but there is no other way. We cannot challenge their authority unless we challenge their authority. We know we can technically revert to the old style of elections. All the laws we need already exist – admittedly not many people know how elections used to work but we can teach them – I digress. Success can only be achieved if we can prove more people want to vote for their leaders than want the Department Assembly to remain."

He didn't appear to be saying anything new and she started making a winding-up gesture with her hand, mindful it had been about thirty seconds.

"OK, I'll get to the point. I spoke to the Chief Justice. Protest isn't illegal but it is illegal to enter the CBD without a permit. So…." He was about to burst and she still had no idea what he was talking about. "Human chain! Human chain around the City. It's perfect! There will be no large groups which will hopefully stop the crowd effect so they can't bring in a rule preventing crowds or gatherings and they won't be able to arrest everyone at the same time so most people will be able to escape!"

He looked to be completely invested in this idea and she appreciated how sincerely he had considered the safety of her people. She had potatoes in the oven.

"This is getting closer to an idea I might like. Now please go home. I will put out some feelers and if I get any positive responses we can talk details."

He looked like he was about to launch into another monologue so she leapt out the swing, ran inside and closed the door on him. Blowing a kiss, she waved goodbye through the window.

45

The layers of wall coverings in April's office had finally began to resemble the cosiness of her pre-destruction décor. Except now she was surrounded by her own work and pictures of people she loved. She'd graduated the Accelerated Junior Leadership Program with honours which she was later told indicated she was on a pathway to Department Manager. This may have been exciting if the Department wasn't in disarray. As gossip of a return to democracy spread through the building, the Department Managers in Department East had done their best to reassure the staff their offices were secure which contrarily backfired; people interpreted their acknowledgement as confirmation the rumours were true. The edgy employees at Department East, acutely aware they were housed in the old Parliament building, were worried about their jobs and becoming unproductive and uncooperative. April could not have envisaged a time when her colleagues would unashamedly talk back to a Department

Manager, but they had spiralled and irrationally resolved they had nothing left to lose.

Her engagement, and every moment spent with her fiancé, was perfect but her post-proposal elation soon dissipated when Patrice and Lidia ended their friendship. It was strange, like a breakup neither really wanted. Patrice promised she would make a concession so they could both attend April's wedding but it was tiring to have to pretend the other didn't exist and consequently she drifted from both. Between the wedding planning and her recent promotion following her graduation, she didn't have time to miss them and – seeking to avoid Lidia's activism – she became more involved with her friends in maths and her fiancé's friends in engineering.

April's colleagues were worried about the politicisation of their work. They presently had almost no oversight and total autonomy over the direction of their research. Subject to the Department Assembly approving their proposals and providing funding, they mostly solved problems they identified through the data they collected and analysed. She regularly arrived at lunch to find them talking about how awful it would be to have to investigate what someone who had no idea about engineering or maths decided you should research. They couldn't understand how they would even do research without their own discretion to follow the patterns the data presented. They were determinedly against any change and couldn't see any benefits to altering the way they worked, citing systems which, after decades of improvement, were essentially faultless.

April, having embraced her new status as a future Department Manager, took to the archives and arranged for a panel of octogenarians who had been researchers before formation to come and talk to them. She also secretly hated the idea of having to do research that someone else told her to do and wanted to be reassured. The panel was a sensation and they realised how many of the assumptions they had made were wrong. Back then, data was available to everyone so anyone could do research and if you wanted to do your own research you didn't have to work for government. The panel explained with affection that most people who did research before the Department worked in universities and research companies who were paid by the government for their work. The session revived the mood in the building. Persistent despair was replaced with an excitement that perhaps change could be even better than they had ever imagined. While thankful for their insights, April doubted it, but was glad to see her friends smiling again.

46

Patrice arranged to work from her apartment under the Dome so she could see whether anyone attended the event. The Human Chain Project had been advertised for over a month after lawyers for 'The Chain' advised the Department Assembly of the intention of their anonymous clients to hold a peaceful protest. The Department Assembly consented. In addition to not really knowing how they would be able to stop it, the protest would be a good opportunity to see whether all the fuss and drama Clifton had been creating had any substance. It was the intention that participants would sit in a chain around the CBD for five hours to symbolise the five decades the City had been in chains. Patrice requested the Dome not waste any resources on this matter as she knew it was Clifton and Lidia who were behind the ominous organisation. She did ask the Chief Operator to do some calculations; he reported one ring of the CBD would require about six thousand people.

The Human Chain was magnificent. Somehow they had coordinated their protest outfits to align with the street grid blocks and, having trickled in over the morning, by the start time the CBD looked like it was wearing a scarf. The road carriageways were completely full of people who had brought chairs and blankets casually encasing the CBD. They played music and sang and ate, exploring their sections, making new friends and introducing each other to people they knew. It was spectacularly civil and, as gently as they had arrived, they gradually filtered back out into the suburbs; with the exception of some rubbish and chalk drawings on the road, they left no trace and did no damage.

The Dome estimated close to five hundred thousand people attended. Patrice was unsurprised that Lidia's gravitas combined with the intrigue of Clifton's defection had emboldened such a turnout. 'The Chain' had no demands but she was aware from the Chief Operator that Clifton would shortly be launching the 'End Date, Election Date' campaign on the back of their success which would require the Department to respond. She spent the day in awe of their progress and was compelled to hasten the Department Assembly's resolve.

Patrice asked her groundskeeper to select some cuttings from the Rose Garden and sent Lidia a vase with the flowers, some photos of the protest from their roof top security cameras and a card which read: 'I don't negotiate with terrorists…. but I would like to see you and Clifton promptly in my office!'

47

Patrice hadn't needed to dominate a meeting in quite some time but the Department Managers, while aware the Human Chain Project was happening, were not prepared for the outpouring of support for Lidia and Clifton and had started to panic. Before the protest, a few Department Managers had joked about how embarrassed they felt for Clifton having thrown away his career to sit in the street and commented how pathetic it would be if they weren't able to complete the chain. Patrice had not divulged Lidia's network to the Dome or Department Managers and they were consequently shocked by the opposition they'd been able to generate in such a short time. Their petulance was unbecoming and they required realigning. She stood in front of a gaunt-faced room, summoned her fiercest tone and started the meeting.

"As you are all by now aware Clifton and Lidia were the instigators of the Human Chain Project which attracted over five hundred thousand people. While admittedly disruptive, it was a peaceful and uneventful protest. Quite an achievement on their part. We have intelligence this symbolic demonstration was their first event. They have signalled their strength. They have more events planned. Next time they will have demands." A shudder rippled across the room. She lowered her voice.

"You know Clifton and he won't stop until he has achieved his goal. You all know how determined he is." They nodded in unison. "I have thought long and consulted widely and I don't think his approach achieves what he desires. I have invited him and Lidia to meet with me next week and will give them an opportunity to present their case. I will not have them running around the City like renegades. If they want something from us they can come here and ask for it." Heads nodded and approving grunts and claps rung out. She moved from her spot at the front of the room and walked closer toward them.

"I know you all understand the depth and complexity of these issues which have been before us for some time. I know some of you agree with Clifton, some of you disagree with him and some of you are open to considering any arguments put to you in the course of your responsibilities to the Department Assembly." She caught the eyes of the Department Managers she suspected had been in contact with Clifton, who were, as usual, smirking.

"They will not stop until there is a resolution either way. I am not in this role to pass judgement on whether there is a right or wrong path for us to take. I am here, however, to make one thing plain." She placed her hands on the table in front of her and leaned in.

"If you want to follow in Clifton's footsteps, if you want to be a politician, you should resign now and join him. You can't be both. If, at the end of this, the Parliament is resurrected the politicians will do the work we do here. They will decide what is in the best interests of this City, not us. If you believe in a return to democracy you must, as Clifton did, walk away from the Department Assembly and help him to build a political class."

She gave them some time to digest the ultimatum. She thought she knew who would go, but these extraordinary minds kept their true desires hidden well beneath the surface.

"I expect to see resignations on my desk by the end of the week. Political leadership takes courage. The first step is out the door."

48

The rumour mill had just about fallen off its hinges and Patrice feared if Lidia and Clifton walked into the Department together it would certainly collapse. Preventatively, she arranged with the Dome to host their meeting at Government House and they agreed but cautioned discretion was required. She was relieved the Chief Operator allowed the meeting at Government House, as Lidia hadn't met her baby daughter yet.

Lidia arrived early to spend some time with Patrice and, once Clifton joined them, Patrice advised the meeting would be recorded and they proceeded outside to the Rose Garden. She was sure Clifton would be grateful as he surely missed a garden, cooped up in the Lamasery. There were to be no refreshments, she wasn't expecting them to stay long.

"Thank you both for coming. I wish the visit was not under such precarious circumstances but knowing you both personally I feel we can have a frank discussion about the practicalities of the situation without the need for accusations. I will provide a summary of events to hasten us to the point, so we can focus on discussing the matters which bring us together today." They nodded.

"First, I know you were both instrumental in the Human Chain Project. This was not illegal but as you are aware, if we wanted to stop you, we would have. I appreciate the affable way in which your lawyers liaised with the Department before and after the event. It is clear from the volume of people who attended you have strong support and I recognise your leadership and your supporters' belief in you. We do not need to discuss this matter." They nodded.

"Secondly, I know you are planning a campaign titled 'End Date, Election Date'. This may be illegal. I don't have much information about what you are planning. Having been present for the first part of Clifton's journey, I assume this slogan is based on the legal advice Clifton has internalised which sets out the legalities of returning Parliament by inserting an end date into the Formation Agreement, and simultaneously scheduling an election on that date." They looked forlorn and nodded.

"Thank you for being honest about your plans so we can proceed to my view on this matter and if necessary a discussion." Lidia had not met this version of Patrice and was reminded of their first brunch at Rippon Lea Estate, arresting and chilling.

"I do not believe, on the evidence I have reviewed to date, your approach aligns with your values." They were startled, wishing her to be incorrect. "The method by which you seek, essentially, a reversion to democracy is not, in itself, democratic. I understand you want to go back to democracy because you prefer that style of governance but the choice is not between two fictional political parties that do not exist. The choice is between the Department Assembly and you." Clifton sank into his chair. Patrice ignored his change in posture. Lidia held her breath.

"I have considered along with all the nostalgia about freedom and self-determination the horror of those who suffered atrocities before formation. A decision by the Department Assembly to revert to democratic elections, in the manner you suggest, denies the people who do not want to revive the old ways the opportunity to defend the life they have now. If you actually believed in giving the people the right to choose the style of governance of this City, the first choice is between the Department Assembly and the Parliament."

They sat in silence while she gave them time to regain their composure then continued softly. "I appreciate from your perspective you are seeking to work within existing legal frameworks, the old and the current. However we have a duty to the people of this City to disband with our assumptions and let them decide what they want. Lidia, you once told me the laws weren't the problem, it was the people. Without political parties there is no choice. The people they trust are sitting around this table."

She reached out and took their hands. "I am willing to reinstate the Parliament if that is what people want. But we have to know they believe again, be certain the wounds have healed and that everyone understand the mistakes. You both taught me the lessons of that time. We cannot consider moving forward until they have a real choice."

Lidia was overcome with pride at her friend's profound understanding of her duty. Patrice did not want them to speak, lest they accidentally confess to a crime surrounded by microphones and hurried to end the meeting.

"I invited you here today to ask you to stop your campaign. Work with me and the Department. I don't want to see your energy wasted trying to find loopholes and sneaky tricks to force an outcome impatiently which may not be the best outcome for everyone. Let's take our time and do this together."

49

Diamond watched the woman he once wanted to marry agree to marry someone else. He had been allowed out of prison for the ceremony by stating on his application that April was his sister. She visited him without fail once a month even though the experience was so stressful she would sweat profusely and run out the room when their time concluded. Lying to be there for her was the least he could do when she had been so faithful to him, even after his actions caused her so much anguish. He joked to Lidia that the worst they could do was put him in prison who, unimpressed, retorted that apparently corrections had not corrected him yet. It was wonderful to be in Lidia's company again; he missed their time together.

Today April was far more beautiful than he remembered but the romantic feelings which once consumed him had long been replaced by the enduring love for his treasured friend now coursing through him. He had never been to a wedding and found the vows extremely awkward. Neither April nor her husband were soppy people and they looked self-conscious as they spoke of their unconditional love for each other. He was interested to learn they were getting married in the State Library because they first kissed on the steps in the moonlight on the way home after staying back, both prolonging their study, so they could be alone after their friends left. A move which her husband later confessed he had planned for weeks. Diamond had assumed they were getting married at a library because they were both equally studious. It wouldn't have surprised him if they'd been married at Department East.

The ceremony ended and April blushed as they kissed and the crowd cheered through tears. The moment they disappeared back down the aisle, the officer who had accompanied him signalled they needed to go. He hugged Lidia, dropped the letter he'd written for April with her father and was promptly whisked back to prison.

50

On the fifty year anniversary Patrice introduced the most extensive reforms since formation. The paradigm had shifted and
everyone inside the Department and out had become heightened
to their own potential. As curiosity mounted, Patrice had recognised they needed to adapt and nurture this growing confidence.

As provoked, fourteen Department Managers had confronted their ambition and resigned. She was blindsided when
her husband turned up in her office with a grin and a resignation letter. The Justice Portfolio had been an awakening for him
and he wanted to use his profile and influence to become an
advocate for youth crime prevention. The senselessness of the
ruined lives which – if for a small amount of attention – could
have avoided had been hard for him to cope with and she was, as
usual, impressed by his fortitude. She suspected also he wanted
to spend more time with their daughter with whom he was
besotted; he had resented their work hours since she was born.

Accepting the resignations, Patrice demoted a further twenty-one Department Managers and promoted seven of the younger generation who, as a result of the long tenures, had been locked out of decision making. Over time, the portfolios had become too specialised and many of the Department Managers who'd held portfolios for decades had become cut-off from what was happening broadly and in other teams. In recognition of the role outside leadership was expected to play moving forward, the Department Assembly was halved to thirty-one including the Department Secretary as the casting vote. The new Department Assembly was agile, nimble and more diverse and its members more engaged; with fewer voices each member was more accountable for their influence on every decision taken.

Department East hadn't been effectual as a facility for some time. Regardless of the reassurances of Department Managers, the historical significance of the building was a distraction and unsettled the brilliant minds within who were not functioning to their normally high capacity. It was eventually conceded the staff would need to be relocated and new high security labs were built in Geelong; everyone else was relocated throughout existing facilities. April was content to find herself a new home at Department Central in an upper level office with a giant floor to ceiling window boasting an excellent view down to the State Library. Once the relocation was complete, the Department Managers who had resigned to pursue careers as politicians were given offices in Department East, as well as Lidia, Clifton and a number of well-known community leaders of calibre.

Patrice had, in concert with the Chief Justice, resolved that in order for there to be any genuine choice for the City as to its form of government, they first needed to have a pool of capable leaders. Therefore, leadership would need to be cultivated; there would need to be space for a leadership base to establish lawfully and grow legitimately. Clifton and Lidia slowly came to terms with the fact that in their lifetime they may not see a return to democracy but were heartened that, should the time come that the political class could provide a product the people trusted, the Department Assembly would not obstruct the transition. They reluctantly, but with wisdom, abandoned their activism and accepted the alternative honour that the Department wished to bestow upon them, embracing with enthusiasm their new mandate to build a political class.

Although the Chief Justice was concerned with the lack of formality or merit surrounding the allocation of Department East, Patrice resolved they had to start somewhere. It was in the hands of the 'politicians' whether they would be able to coordinate and organise themselves into something resembling a government. In exchange for their offices in Department East, they were expected to use the chambers to host meetings and gatherings and seek opinions from the community. She emphasised the importance of using their leadership to advance knowledge of parliamentary democracy but felt it vital to their development that the Department Assembly have no formal influence over their operations. Their independence was paramount.

The Chief Justice was uncomfortable and drafted an annex to the Governance Rules outlining their responsibilities ready to be adopted by the Department Assembly, as she phrased it, 'the second this goes horribly awry'. Patrice doubted she could give them free reign forever but wanted to allow them to come to her, in their own time, with their own parameters. She saw no point in undermining them from the outset.

The changes to the governance of the City were profound and she felt a lightness spread throughout the Department as it took its new form as open and welcoming instead of the fortress it had become. The changes, however, were intangible and on the anniversary day, as a visible gesture of gratitude and respect, the Department Assembly removed the checkpoints to the CBD, disbanded permits and ungated the lanes. The Dome advised that with the politicians now located in Department East, the threat level was significantly reduced. The Chief Operator had subsequently supported easing restrictions with caution. He took Patrice aside and told her how proud he was of her and that she was doing a wonderful job. There were few people she respected more, his praise both generous and reaffirming.

The opening of the lanes was Clifton's suggestion. Their Human Chain Project had been a catalyst. Five hours of fusion of the previously unconnected bohemian underbelly sparked a rebirth of drama and collaboration and music and ignited creativity which thereafter had no outlet. Clifton, perpetually annoyed by the wasted beauty of the empty shopfronts, grasped the opportunity for a resurgence of the arts in the lanes. This, Patrice ruminated, was the heart of political leadership. She found his arguments and conviction compelling and was charmed by his commitment to the Arts Precinct's success. The edge the City had been missing, he exclaimed.

51

Lidia sat at her office window and watched her fellow aspiring politicians bickering in the courtyard below. Their first week at Department East had gotten off to a rough start but they'd quickly found a rhythm. The original Parliament building had been converted into public meeting rooms and conference rooms and the later addition at the rear had been allocated exclusively for their private use. They arrived on Monday, were handed access passes, given a security and safety briefing and a tour of the building, and then left to their own devices.

The process of selecting offices left her afraid their ambitions had been ill-founded. They'd been given nothing from the Department other than the building. As the sliding doors closed and the officials disappeared, they'd stood for a brief moment speechless, not quite sure what to do next. Lidia, in a feeble attempt to break the awkward silence, said jokingly she should get the best office because she was the oldest. This lead to a discussion about which was the best office, how they would decided who would get an office if several people wanted the same one, what would be the fairest method, how would they make sure everyone got an office they liked and so on; an hour later they were still standing in the foyer, now screaming at one another. Thankfully a leader emerged.

Patrice's husband sent everyone outside to the courtyard while he found some stationary. He numbered the offices, distributed pencils and paper and told everyone to inspect all the offices and choose five which would be acceptable, after which they were to reconvene for a negotiation in the courtyard. When they resurfaced, numbers in hand, he had devised a debate style tribunal whereby they started with the most highly sought after office and worked their way backwards. Each person vying for an office was given one minute to pitch to the others why they deserved the office and then the courtyard would vote. The person with the most votes would get the office, no appeals. Lidia's favourite was the last north facing first floor office, farthest from the entrance at the end of the courtyard. It had the best light and views. Fortunately, she was able to successfully argue her case against three others who had drawn the same conclusion. However, because they were all involved in the 'Office Tribunal', no one could leave to go to their hard won office and by the end of the day everyone had an office they liked but had achieved nothing else.

Anna's wealth meant Lidia had never had to work and in spite of all her time spent leading others, she'd never had an office. Her first act was to place a sign she'd made in the shed on the door stating: 'No Pot Plants'. The farm was overrun with pot plants and she needed to prevent the tradition catching on. Lidia had found the first week exciting but overwhelming. Her presence in the building was bittersweet and as with every milestone, her success on the journey was always juxtaposed with her loss. During her years at the Lamasery she missed Anna intensely and the loop of their conversations ran continuously in her head, matched to the dull ache in her heart. This pain was different. No one in Bendigo knew Anna but here many had met her as an athlete and everyone who entered her office had their own recollections: the new memories of her both precious and excruciating. She hoped she wouldn't need to make a sign saying: 'Don't Talk About Anna'.

It was Clifton's idea while they were getting to know each other that they convene in the courtyard each morning and have a coffee and plan their day; so the ritual was born and by the week's end loose priorities started to emerge out of their ramblings. Lidia, unlike the others, immediately begun utilising the conference rooms and already had many people booked in to see her, withdrawing from their daily gathering early to get to her meetings. Others, a bit bewildered, spent almost all day in the courtyard at first but as ideas flowed, like magnets, they were naturally forming clusters. The breadth of concerns and matters which they pondered was impressive. Some were interested in buildings and infrastructure, others were interested in people and improving quality of life, some were concerned with the practicalities of their coordination. Patrice's husband, concerned with the relentless courtyard procrastination, insisted they develop a schedule of tasks which they should all contribute to completing and then allocate the rest of the time to pursue their individual interests.

They agreed anecdotally their biggest barrier was that very few people had experienced voting in an election.

Correspondingly, they designed an information session which explained the basics of a parliamentary democracy and took turns to host interested guests in the chambers, encouraged by surging demand. Clifton explained they needed to learn the old laws and then decide whether to write completely new laws, so they implemented a Law Working Group. Similarly, the Chief Justice offered to teach them the Parliamentary Rule Book, after which they would need to decide whether they wanted to keep or rewrite it. The weekly commitments shrunk Lidia's calendar significantly but the structure made them all more productive and decisive; the functional knowledge acquired invaluable. They were drawing attention and criticism; their following growing faster than anyone had anticipated.

52

April was early to meet Lidia for dinner and diverted to the bench outside her old office at Department East while she waited. She could hear a discussion through the open window. She thought one of the voices sounded like Clifton and they were talking about setting up a sculpture studio and hoped he would be able to assist securing a lease. She resented having to move to Department Central. She'd loved her office at Department East and the old building encircled by beautiful gardens and missed this peaceful side of the City. It was busy at Department Central and harder to concentrate. She'd been appointed to the Department Assembly as a Junior Manager. This meant she didn't have a portfolio but was still expected to vote. The role diminished her ability to focus on her statistical work and, depending on the day, she either loved or hated the responsibility. She loathed being distracted by the attention she received but Patrice refused to let her quit, every time she complained enrolling her in another training course to address her latest frustration.

The past few weeks had been particularly absurd when she got her turn on the rumour mill. Someone had found out she was Anna's niece which she hadn't realised was a secret. She talked about Lidia frequently, but it seemed she had never specifically mentioned Lidia had been Anna's wife. April didn't think this was deceptive as she'd never met Anna and didn't know anything about her but the furore from her friends and the subsequent ripple through the Department was ridiculous. It was particularly painful when she overheard two of her supposed close girlfriends muttering it hadn't made sense that she had been made a Junior Manager because she was nothing special, but it all made sense now that they knew the truth. She was devastated and Patrice assured April, through her tears, that was absolutely not the case and she was appointed to the Department Assembly because she was a brilliant diagnostician and they valued her input. April was looking forward to seeing Lidia, the only person other than her husband and Patrice who was not disgusted at her apparent betrayal.

Later, Patrice remembered she had encouraged April to join the Accelerated Junior Leadership Program as a ruse to meet her and felt a pang of guilt. Perhaps April was extraordinary because she was genetically part Anna but her talent was nonetheless her own and Patrice would never stop pushing her – still consumed by her doubts – to see herself as a leader. Fame was absolutely not worth it April had declared earlier; Patrice immediately enrolled her in a course about accepting things you cannot change.

Shortly after moving into her office at Department East, Lidia had started visiting Anna's grave after work to try to consolidate and release her pain. April had never been. It was coming up to the anniversary of Anna's death and Lidia had been struggling, her grief was so raw it was like she had just died. At dinner, April finally understood why Lidia was having such a hard time – she'd met someone. She was the sister of one of the Department Managers who resigned to become a politician and they had run into each other a few times at events and struck up a friendship. Lidia wanted more and knew she couldn't avoid the chemistry between them much longer but wasn't coping with the guilt of deserting Anna. The angst was making her emotional which was draining her energy and she was snapping at everyone. She was falling in love with this woman and her eyes sparkled when she described their time together. April was confronted by the complexity of the feelings Lidia was experiencing but was excited at the prospect of seeing her aunt happy. April reached over the table and took her hand. Lidia had tears in her eyes.

"I honestly don't know what to do. I love Anna, I love her like she is still alive."

"You know people are always telling me I am exactly like her."

Lidia laughed. "You are very like her, but without any athletic ability—at all!" As was proven when constructing the shed and she could barely lift a hammer.

"If I am exactly like Anna it stands to reason I think like she would think and if I was her, this is what I would say—" April sat up straight and attempted to imitate a person she'd never met. "Lidia, a beautiful woman wants to date you. I'm dead. Get on with it!"

They both dissolved into laughter and tears of relief spilled onto Lidia's cheeks. "That is absolutely what she would have said."

They finished dinner and Lidia took her to the cemetery and introduced April to her aunt. Then said goodbye.

53

Patrice was heartened by how well the politicians had been getting on. They initially had an enormous number of rowdy disagreements, usually over important matters, and frequently ended up in her office. She turned them away stating if they were running the City, there would be no one else to solve their problems so they had better sort it out; only to have them return the next day with a different problem to which she provided the same answer. Fearing the neediness would never end – and mindful of the conflict of her involvement in their daily deliberations – she coaxed the former Chief Justice out of retirement and appointed him as an in-house mediator, relieved to be rid of them.

By all accounts, their presence, however audacious, was having a positive impact. Their initiatives were not intrusive and people who wanted to explore their exhibits enjoyed the experience. They were igniting passions all over the City. Ever sensational, they called themselves the 'First Politicians' and their following was growing steadily and, according to the Dome, responsibly.

Their popularity had recently sparked anti-democratic groups who, staunchly against any change to the Department Assembly, held a protest on the Department East steps chanting 'Democracy Kills, Department Rules'. Patrice suspected the protesters didn't grasp the irony. Nevertheless, imagining the Chief Justice's raised eyebrow, Patrice resolved it was time to consider where this was going and requested the First Politicians nominate someone to represent them; they chose Clifton.

She invited him to meet her in the Rose Garden at Government House knowing how much he'd adored his roses. He responded that he would prefer to meet on neutral ground. She should have anticipated this level of drama from such a prolific strategist and was amused at the image of them sitting around for hours plotting that move. She was already bored with the game. She told him affectionately to pick the place and stop being annoying or she would shut them down. He was coy but chuffed at the victory. He was going to be mischievous and propose that they meet at the Werribee Rose Garden, but wisely resisted the jest. Clifton knew she loved the foreshore and recommended some early morning exercise before breakfast in Williamstown. Her daughter slept as they walked and talked.

"At present you don't cost me anything. The staff couldn't work in Department East because they felt unsafe, you are all self-funded and the officials who run the building would be doing so regardless of which community groups were using the space. Therefore the burden of you continuing in perpetuity is very little to the Department and, by all accounts, the First Politicians are having a stimulating effect on the City." Clifton was pleased with Patrice's positive outlook, albeit a little hurt by her dismissive summary of their transformational influence.

"Nevertheless, you are not doing all this work to maintain statis and there will come a time where you will either prosper or fizzle." She may as well have slapped him, he had been expecting her to tell him how wonderful they all were. She seemed to view them as a charming nuisance.

"As I stated when we lent you Department East, should you be able to organise yourselves and the people wanted to return the Parliament, we would be open to facilitating that transition." He was encouraged.

"Therefore, I want to ensure we have the same understanding of the parameters which would satisfy the Department Assembly in order for that transition to occur." Patrice had spent time with the Chief Justice working through the legal and ethical issues at length. The Chief Justice was satisfied the First Politicians were taking their lessons seriously and was impressed by the promising ingenuity of their suggestions.

"The Department is not a political organisation. A democratic election is not between the Department and the First Politicians. A return to a democratically elected Parliament would see the Department Assembly dissolved and the Department would become accountable to the Parliament instead of being accountable to the Department Assembly. Assuming you intend one day to petition for an election, my concern is the First Politicians do not appear to be splitting into political parties."

Clifton had been having similar discussions with his advisors. Lidia had her network which operated as it always had but still hadn't formalised. The rest had their areas of interest and friendship groups had formed naturally within the building but they worked together on most things. Patrice's husband had become the de facto leader concerning the operation of the building, however there had been no heartfelt attempts at separating ideologically. Patrice waited for him to respond and when he didn't continued, "I am informed by the Chief Justice you are working through the old laws and many have followed Lidia's lead and are using the old electoral maps as the basis for establishing the boundaries of their community liaisons." He nodded.

He didn't realise the Chief Justice was spying on them and was annoyed with himself for not realising sooner that she would have been keeping Patrice informed of their progress. Patrice clearly assumed he, as an ex-Department Secretary, would have known she was kept apprised of their improvements given he was fully aware of the Dome's protocols. On their first day at Department East it wasn't a coincidence all the former Department Managers selected offices on the north side of the building with south facing windows; out of the direct view line of the Dome's cameras.

"Your advancement is primarily dependent on the First Politicians' ability to demonstrate there are two political parties with enough candidates for one candidate in every electorate in both houses. Until such a time, we will consider you as a community organisation." She stopped walking and turned to face him and put her hand on his arm.

"You don't have to convince me you should be in Government. You need to convince the people. Even if we give you an election, we can't make them vote. I can't make them believe in you. You have to do that yourself. When you are ready, you will have one chance, make sure you don't waste it."

54

Lidia'd had the luxury of getting to know her custodians over many years and some over decades but most of them had never met each other. From her first day at Department East, she'd started to disclose them to one another in pairs. She introduced each one to at least one adjoining custodian then began forming smaller groups based on geography. Once she was satisfied they were all excited and committed to a political career, she planned their first party meeting.

The custodians were fused by their shared past; however Lidia was mindful of the array of personalities and was nervous that while they had democracy in common, many of them would have nothing else. She invited them to the farm for a full day of activities and strategy planning sessions. Clifton had come to help transform the house into a conference centre and they crammed the living room with plastic seats, whiteboards and snacks.

The agenda was to select a name for their party and settle on its shared values which would underpin their policy platforms into the future. Concerned some of the overbearing custodians would come with a list, she'd not given them notice of the task. She wanted them to come to their consensus together from start to finish as a team, as they would need to if they were leading the City. It was an inspiring day. Their enthusiasm and positivity was contagious and their encouragement of each other and the respect with which they considered and criticised ideas was far more dignified than the courtyard sledging she was used to. She was immensely proud of their approach to solving the task and at the end of the day they unanimously adopted their values statement and left, united and determined.

To announce the establishment of their party, Lidia arranged for a photo to be taken of them in their corresponding seats in the old Legislative Assembly Chamber. The image was tremendously evocative and provoked the ex-Department Managers into action. They had been required to vacate their Department Estates but had remained living in their local communities and were well known and popular. It didn't take long, given their extensive networks, for elites and celebrities to fill the remaining seats and their party was complete.

In his capacity as 'First Politicians Representative', Patrice invited Clifton to join the Department Assembly. He had no vote but was privy to most of their discussions with the exception of security items and this connection between the Department Assembly and the First Politicians worked well. Patrice was pregnant again and her husband didn't want to stand as a candidate as he intended to be at home with the new baby and decided instead to run their party organisation.

This suited him and allowed him to focus on his youth crime prevention advocacy. Lidia was relieved. He was so enigmatic, no one would have been able to beat him. He had approached Clifton who was still living at the Lamasery – which technically didn't exist – to join them as their representative in the Legislative Assembly. Lidia had also asked Clifton to join her party as a representative in the Legislative Council. He was content spending his time in the lanes, advocating for artists and liaising with the Department, and was disinclined to join either party. The First Politicians were slowly winning hearts. Patrice expected it wouldn't be long until sentiments started to shift.

55

Clifton had been timorous at the thought of returning to the Department Assembly. His fellow First Politicians had rallied behind him so emphatically though, he couldn't bring himself to confess the circumstances under which he had stormed out the building. Patrice, tickled at his remorse, assured him the forum was completely different and not to worry about the past, which he couldn't change.

As promised, he found his hesitations were one sided and the fresh enthusiastic new group were inviting and encouraging and enjoyed hearing tales of the events and projects brewing at Department East. It would never have occurred to him to restructure the Department Assembly and he wondered ruefully whether his resignation had been the best thing to ever happen to them.

All property in the lanes had been acquired by the Department when they had been gated. When the Department reopened the lanes, as negotiated by Clifton, the empty shops were designated for use by artists. There was a plethora of paperwork required to secure one of these coveted spaces and the arts community descended upon Clifton to advocate on their behalf, itching to be part of the new Arts Precinct.

Patrice, while not putting any pressure on him at the Department Assembly meetings, had expectations Clifton was keeping the First Politicians in line and he was careful to demonstrate their collegiality whenever possible. Since her husband had joined the ex-Department Managers exclusively, some of the stragglers at Department East had gotten sloppy. No one had realised how much work he had been doing to keep everyone to the schedule. As a result, Clifton scaled back his involvement in the Arts Precinct to take over managing Department East.

The two parties had started to drift in separate directions. Patrice was satisfied with the current arrangements and would not be intervening again, leaving Clifton to consider their prospects. He often retreated to the old Parliament Library in Department East to ponder. It was rarely occupied and its towering walls of books stuffed with wisdom inspired him to think deeply about their trajectory. Their divergence caused him concern but he'd been unable to discern why and was committed to meditating on his trepidation.

He eventually resolved, in order for the Department Assembly to agree to an election, they would need to be satisfied both parties were equally capable of governing the City. He was worried their gradual parting may result in an imbalance which would undermine the integrity of their joint objective. He felt it was premature at this juncture for them to become independent of each other while they were still contemplating the detail of how a future Parliament might function; a task they would need to resolve together. In order for one to succeed they must both succeed. He was certain this high-quality thinking was only possible in the presence of rare and precious books and set about planning a presentation to explain this revelation and offer a strategy to ensure they were growing together as well as apart.

Clifton gathered the First Politicians in the courtyard and shared his observations that he was concerned their development was progressing at different rates. He explained they both had a vested interest in each other's advancement and highlighted that, without the other, neither had any prospects. Therefore, it was in both their best interests to spend more time working together and sharing resources on matters on which there was agreement; this would also assist to better accentuate their differences to potential future voters. He also encouraged them to work together to develop strategies to convince the Department Assembly to hold an election. They were receptive and grateful for his guidance and he felt relieved he had been able to refocus their attention to the monumental task they had ahead of them.

56

Lidia lay in bed grinning as she gazed at the trees outside her window and listened to her lover singing in the kitchen as she made breakfast. It was bliss to be back at the farm. They spent most of their time during the week at her terrace in Brunswick but given Lidia's fame, they never relaxed in the City. Due to the familial connection to one of her rivals, Lidia had insisted on a politics ban in the relationship. Consequently, their romance revolved around art and food, a separation for which Lidia was especially grateful after the mind-bending feat of trying to understand how ministers had been appointed.

The Chief Justice was endlessly patient with the First Politicians as they struggled to understand how a cabinet was the peak decision-making forum but technically didn't exist; and that you wouldn't know who you could pick until after the election because your best team member for the job may not win their seat. It was baffling and, ultimately, the Chief Justice told them for the sake of their sanity, she would postpone this lesson. Instead she gave them a list of ministerial portfolios to appoint so they could formalise seniority within their ranks and get experience working in a hierarchy.

Lidia didn't feel comfortable making that decision herself and allowed her party to nominate and vote for who they wanted in the positions. Because Lidia wasn't confident she could explain to her custodians how a cabinet worked, voting took place under the erudite guidance of the Chief Justice who graciously agreed to assist in her free time. She reminded them throughout that this was not how anyone would actually have appointed a cabinet, but she was happy they were happy.

Once both parties appointed their cabinets, coordinating with the senior members of each group streamlined decision making and their efficiency progressed exponentially. Under Clifton's direction, they met regularly to debate community concerns and issues of which one or both of their cabinets had become aware; this interaction helped them to determine their shared values and identify the matters on which they decisively disagreed.

Clifton was satisfied with their progress and called them to the courtyard for a strategy meeting. He was pleased with their comprehensive knowledge and from his perspective felt they were evenly matched in their capacity to provide a high level of service to the community, albeit noting their very different approaches. Soon, they would need to turn their attention to convincing the Department Assembly to call an election. Consequently they would need to consider what type of evidence would compel the Department Assembly to agree. He suggested they explore the question separately and bring their recommendations to the next meeting as they would need to work together to commit to a long term strategy if they were to be prepared to request an election at the same time. Clifton reminded them, 'You are running in the same race, you have the same finish line, there is no race if you aren't both present when the starting gun is fired'.

Lidia was thinking of ways they could prove to Patrice the people wanted her to be their Premier when she became pleasantly preoccupied with tea and toast.

57

April arrived home to find her dinner in the oven and a long letter waiting for her on the dining table.

She and her husband had been moved out of their apartment and into Rippon Lea Estate when she became a Junior Manager. They had been given the choice between this home, Tasma Terrace or Waller House. It was a childhood dream that her father would become a Department Manager and they would move to Como House with its glorious verandah but it was occupied. April was familiar with Rippon Lea Estate from Patrice's dinner parties and the responsibility of running an estate was daunting enough without having to worry about whether they would like the property. It took her longer to get home than when they lived in Carlton and, with her late nights becoming more frequent, her husband was often asleep before she got home. He had started leaving letters for her to read over her dinner.

She loved reading his thoughts and musings. It seemed the format inspired him to tell her his dreams and express his gratitude for their life and his passion for her. He missed their evenings together and she knew his complaints were not critical but full of longing for their less complicated lives. He would tell her about his day and describe the adventures they would have together when they were old. It was crushing to read his final sentences, evoking her aching love for him, knowing she couldn't kiss him until the morning. She finished dinner, forced desire out of her mind and continued to work.

The Department had received a written request from the First Politicians via Clifton for the Department to insert an end date into the Formation Agreement and concurrently schedule an election. The request was coupled with trolleys of folders lined with hundreds of thousands of pages of petitions evidencing the community's support for their request; they estimated two thirds of the City. Patrice had presented the request to the Department Assembly to decide collectively on a set of assessment criteria.

A preliminary vote indicated the Department Assembly was split fifteen to fifteen. As the reports and opinions flowed in, they considered the legal perspective, social perspective and every other possible perspective, yet stayed divided. Patrice had been adamant a decision of this importance should not be left to the casting vote and requested the Department Managers get together separately to come to a consensus. They went through three rounds of votes with supplementary concerns necessitating more research and then a further two votes, but the Department Managers remained evenly split. Patrice finally conceded she would need to make the decision and asked each side to nominate a representative to present their case.

April was vehemently against an election and practiced her speech one last time before going to bed. In the morning, she left before her husband woke and headed into the office early so as to avoid her colleagues and barricaded herself in her office until it was time for the speeches to begin. She could feel their eyes on her as she walked through Department Central. Fortunately, everyone was aware what was about to take place and knew better than to distract her.

They had thirty minutes each and their backers sat at either side of the room holding their breath. The affirmative representative spoke first. April thought the other side did a good job of articulating their case. She believed so fervently that her side was right that she wasn't nervous and, before she knew it, her comrade was waving the five-minutes-left warning card. April came to the conclusion. Patrice, soaking up the plethora of complex issues, was fixated on April. She put down her speech and stared into Patrice's eyes. "In summary, the technical and legal arguments, which have been demonstrated vigorously by both sides, compel the Department Secretary to decide against disbanding the Department Assembly at this time.

"This is the heart of the matter. When the Department Assembly was convened the fabric of society had eroded. The First Politicians, we all agree, are making progress towards being able to govern this City. They have shown us people believe in them. Many of them are already community leaders, esteemed and capable within their own communities. No one doubts the affection for them is genuine. What their petition demonstrates is people trust them. What this documentation does not do, is demonstrate they understand the mistakes which led to the desolation of an entire generation.

"Chen asked us to build a City free from fear and free from stress. She did that because she inherited a City which was terrified as a result of the incompetence of its leaders. We have no assurances they will not repeat the mistakes of the past. We have seen no laws including safeguards which guarantee they will not repeat the mistakes of the past. We have seen no documentation as to the operations of their party organisations including safeguards which guarantee they will not repeat the mistakes of the past.

"We would be negligent in our duty to the people of the City to concede to this request prematurely. I respect the arguments of our esteemed colleagues who believe the First Politicians have demonstrated the people want them to lead and that we should respect the will of the people. I wish that the will of the people was enough. I wish the will of the people was strong enough five decades ago to prevent the carnage which nearly razed our City to the ground and resulted in millions of deaths but we know that it wasn't. We know our duty to the people of this City in this deliberation is to ensure, to the best of our ability, future politicians will make laws which take care of everyone. We cannot satisfy that duty today and therefore their request must be denied."

58

Given the decision had ultimately been hers alone, Patrice invited Clifton to the Rose Garden at Government House to give him the outcome in person. She explained the extensive deliberations behind their final reasons for refusing the First Politician's request to schedule an election but wanted him to focus on the steps they could take to resolve the concerns raised. She had sensed he was overconfident and wanted to make sure he understood the preliminary nature of the refusal. He took the news badly and Patrice asked Lidia to check on him when he didn't turn up for his meeting with her husband at Department East the next day.

Lidia arrived at the Lamasery that evening to find Clifton slumped on the window seat. When he noticed she'd let herself in, he grunted and continued to stare out the window. He looked like someone had died. She made him some ginger tea and joined him on the opposite side of the sill.

"Patrice sent me a copy of the letter she gave you last night.

Surely you weren't expecting it to be that easy? I read their reasons. Pretty sensible and open-ended?"

Irritation flashed through him but he caught his tongue before he snapped at her, aware it wasn't Lidia he was angry with. His face softened. "I was certain what we'd provided was enough. Seems hypocritical to imply people don't know what they want after they've told you what they want."

Lidia frowned good-heartedly. "She didn't say that. She said she wanted to see the laws we're proposing to take to an election so they could be confident they would be adequate, given we have no experience and no access to any data relating to the operation of the City. They were impressed with the enormous amount of work we did to get those signatures. I read it as though we are halfway there."

He shrugged and sullenly accepted the praise. "Still. It's hypocritical."

"If you were Patrice would you just hand over the keys to the City? You of all people should appreciate her decision, ex-Department Secretary!" She slapped his shoulder and laughed. He emerged from his pity and let hope return.

"I'm just jealous. She's way better at it than me! You're right. The hard work is done but the Law Working Group hasn't been very effective. Since the parties formed, people have been focused on their own electorates."

Lidia hadn't been part of that group but she didn't think – relative to the petition – it would take long for the laws to be rewritten. She knew her team had been working on their amendments; she wasn't certain about the others. "I'm not sure, but comparatively, I don't think it's a particularly difficult task. We could get new laws drafted fairly quickly."

He lugged himself off the sill and collected the letter from his briefcase. "Looking at this list, theoretically, if we address these issues, the Department Assembly will insert an end date into the Formation Agreement and schedule an election." Lidia began to speak but Clifton, feeling the excitement bubble, interrupted her, "But, but, but…." He started pacing while thinking out loud. "Patrice said something last night which struck me as odd at the time. She wanted to meet me in person because she'd made the casting vote because after five votes they had all voted the same way—fifteen each way every time. That makes me think, no matter what we do, they will always vote the same way." He pointed to Lidia, inviting her opinion.

"That's interesting. No one budged, ever? Sounds like they had their own preconceptions."

"Exactly! So I think what we need to do is appeal this decision to the Court of Justice and demonstrate to the Chief Justice we meet all the criteria in the letter. If we keep going back to the Department Assembly, if they are biased, they will just find new legitimate reasons to reject us. Exactly like Patrice said, they have all the data. We can't prove them wrong!" He sat back down and stared at Lidia waiting for her to agree.

"It sounds sneaky. Even if that is the case, Patrice is still the casting vote. Do you not believe she would support us if she genuinely believed we satisfied these criteria? She doesn't play games like you lot."

He thought about it. "It's not that I don't trust her. We could be going back and forth with the Department for millennia until they're satisfied. They have provided clear reasons here which have simple enough solutions. I just think we have a better chance at success in Court."

She processed his analysis.

"It feels disingenuous to me but I suspect that is because I know Patrice is an honourable woman. If I am Premier one day and I was asked to choose between these options, it would be hard to justify to my constituents passing up the strategy which is most likely to deliver the desired outcome. Still it's not up to us, let's take it to the others tomorrow. We all have a stake in this and they may have different ideas."

59

The Chief Operator requested Patrice visit the Dome for a briefing, not urgently but 'swiftly'. Not knowing what that meant, Patrice cancelled all her meetings, found a tracksuit which barely covered her growing abdomen and snuck out the building. Having not visited in a while it took her longer than normal to remember the secure route but, after a few wrong turns, she arrived at the covert entrance. She dropped by her old colleagues to say hello while she waited for him to finish his meeting.

For privacy, they headed down to her apartment, which Patrice had retained when she became Department Secretary. The kitchen staff brought them coffee and apple tarts. The Chief Operator hadn't wanted to alarm her but the volume of people fuming at the Department Assembly denying the First Politicians' request for an election was concerning. It appeared some of the potential candidates had over-promised what they would do when they were elected and others had not accurately represented what was requested by the First Politicians. The Dome was having trouble keeping on top of the growing hostility towards the Department Assembly and he was taking action to bring in additional staff to process the data.

While they hadn't detected any direct threats he was concerned that, because the Department hadn't been involved in disclosing the request to the citizens, expectations had been mismanaged and he suggested Patrice may want to consider mitigating the fallout before the confusion escalated to violence. He also mentioned his analysts believed it was the intention of the First Politicians to appeal the refusal to the Court of Justice but that they were still considering the optics. Clifton was concerned people who supported retaining the Department Assembly might then refuse to participate in the elections and remained undecided as to how to proceed. The Chief Operator assured Patrice the Dome would keep her updated on any escalations but he wanted her to be aware her intervention could help deter any vengeance. Satisfied with his vigilance, she thanked him for reaching out.

Patrice needed time to think about his advice before she went back to the office and her attention was required elsewhere. She detoured to the lanes. She'd not been to see the restoration since the last of the Arts Precinct vacancies had been filled and could hear the laughter as she walked up the block towards Hardware Lane. She turned the corner to find the narrow pavement swarming with people and navigated the few spaces left between the buildings not occupying visitors. The shopfronts were strewn with artists creating and holding exhibitions and customers exploring their work, randomly collaborating, making music and trading objects they'd made.

By the time she'd squeezed out the other end of the lane, she'd forgotten why she'd come and with a jolt remembered she was supposed to be concerned about terrorists. She felt the excitement radiate from the crowd and, from the safety of the main road, enjoyed their banter as they celebrated each other's creations. The ambiance vibrant and energetic, brimming with positivity.

The First Politicians were making a mess but they had no experience. She reflected there was no other way for them to learn accountability than to answer to those they'd deceived. While the Dome had not detected an actual threat, she was determined not to intervene. They were rebuilding trust and they weren't going to triumph every time but she did need to have a chat with them so they were aware of the negative impact they were having as well as the positive.

Patrice wasn't sure they were transformational yet. Perhaps they felt their presence in everything they touched but from her position there were still many areas of the City unaware of their motivations or the difference between their parties. It was curious her Department Managers had stuck so rigidly to their positions during their deliberations even as the advice changed; unlike most of the decisions they made, none of them was truly impartial. She wondered whether the Court of Justice was a more objective forum for this decision. She'd hoped Clifton would recognise, while they might believe they were ready to govern the City, the City needed some more time. Regardless she couldn't stop them appealing the Department's decision and if they did, the fate of the City would be out of her hands.

Patrice had let time get away from her. The magic of the lanes was captivating and, remembering herself, she turned and sped back to work. How enchanting she thought, as the clamour faded behind her—for now, Clifton was doing something right.

60

The Chief Justice received a request to overturn the Department Assembly's decision to refuse to amend the Formation Agreement. Patrice was informed of the application and requested the matter be expedited to minimise anxiety in the community which had been mounting as fear wrestled excitement.

April was appointed to represent the Department Assembly and sat with their lawyers to provide direction throughout the hearing. The First Politicians sat in the gallery for the duration of the proceedings and Clifton sat with their lawyers on all their behalf.

The Court heard the arguments from both sides. The political parties provided credentials of all potential candidates and their organisational bodies, and statements from signatories to the petition declaring they knew at least one of the candidates intending on running in their electorate and would be satisfied to vote for them. They also provided a list of their respective party membership, the updated laws they would gazette immediately upon being sworn in to replace the Governance Rules and financial accounts showing private funding for the next ten years for each of their organisations.

Surprisingly, both parties wanted to appoint Patrice as Governor once elected and retain the Court of Justice without any changes to its structure. April was aware they were planning to present evidence that all the concerns raised by the Department Assembly had been negated but was unexpectedly impressed at how extensively they'd prepared.

The Department argued the premise of the Formation Agreement was still valid—that the political class was unable to satisfactorily provide leadership to the City. The political parties were still relatively unknown throughout the City and therefore the Department Assembly was unwilling to insert an end date reinstating the political class because they would not be able to provide a higher quality of service for the people of the City than was currently provided by the Department Assembly.

Proceedings lasted two weeks partially due to the persistent interjections from the politicians in the back. The Chief Justice commented as she closed the hearing she couldn't remember a time in her career where she'd had to eject so many people from the gallery, but admitted their passion was affirming. She warned them her deliberation may take some time. She was aware of the stress the uncertainty was causing in their communities but reminded them of the gravitas of their request and asked them to be patient in the interim. April returned to Department Central and updated the Department Assembly after which Patrice and April retreated to the Rose Garden at Government House to debrief.

Patrice had been blindsided when April announced to the Department Assembly that both parties intended to appoint her, if elected, as Governor though relieved they would be able to stay at Government House either way. She dreaded the thought of separating her daughter from the ballroom.

"How did you not know they wanted you to stay on as Governor? You would be an excellent Governor." April was astonished no one had actually asked her before announcing her impending appointment in the Court of Justice. Patrice shook her head in agreed amazement.

"I was just as surprised as everyone else. I hadn't really thought about what I would do. I don't technically have a port-folio like the rest of you. I assumed they would want Clifton in that role. Last I heard the Law Working Group were planning on abolishing the Governor. Maybe they thought the Chief Justice would be more likely to support them if she thought I was still running things." They both laughed. April sighed.

"The whole thing was surreal. They are so reactive and emotional, constantly shouting and screaming opinions. I can't imagine any of them could run the City. They're so intense."

"I know the theatrics can be draining but remember most of them are already in governance. They are extremely capable. Many used to be Department Managers or Local Councillors." She giggled, "They just get frenzied when they're performing!"

April hoped she was right but wished they would try harder to outwardly project order. Their perceived lack of restraint made her nervous.

61

Clifton tapped lightly on Lidia's office door. He was arriving unannounced and didn't want to startle her. She waved him in and he settled on her visitors' couch as she finished the report she was editing. The boisterous nature of their fellow inhabitants in Department East resulted in an outright flouting of the 'No Pot Plants' sign, to the benefit of the courtyard which, once bland, was now awash with beautiful flowers. She had commented that she should have known better than to put a sign on the door. Clifton absolved through chuckles no one had any insight as to the cheek of political camaraderie when they first arrived and not to be so hard on herself.

Ironically, the success of the bustling Arts Precinct had rendered the Lamasery uninhabitable and Clifton relocated to an apartment in Fitzroy. Encouraged by some of his new artistic friends to explore his own creativity, he'd fallen for ceramics and his political ambition had instantly dissipated.

Lidia completed the page and turned to her friend lost day-dreaming out the window. "To what do I owe this pleasure? I see you have a present in that bag. Is it for me?"

He returned to reality. She was peering nosily over the edge of her desk into his shopping bag which contained a box wrapped in sumptuous paper and a giant bow.

"Hello. Yes, it is for you but you can open it after I leave." He took a long breath. "It's a parting gift. I resigned as the First Politician's Representative. I decided to retire." She was stunned.

"What! The Court hasn't even made their decision yet. We could have an election any day. We need to you!" She jumped out her desk chair and joined him on the couch.

"Lidia, I have given my life to this City and I'll continue to mentor and provide guidance but I have other things I want to do now. You don't need me. You know full well these halls are overflowing with talent and every day more people want to become involved. Things are running smoothly here and the First Politician's Representative was always a temporary measure. Soon you won't even need a representative!"

She wanted to contend, but by the tender look on his face, she knew there was no convincing him to stay. He had wildly understated his influence and the others would be devastated but she appreciated after a life of service and the harrowing focus of the recent past he was content with his contribution.

"I will miss you terribly." She hugged him.

He blushed. "You will not because I will be here every second day complaining!"

After reminiscing highlights of their brief but intense friendship, Clifton left to get back to his studio. She unwrapped his gift and found a mug he'd made and engraved 'First Premier'.

62

The Chief Justice called the parties back to the Court to deliver her decision. April sat paralysed in her seat. They'd heard nothing of the deliberations and neither she nor Patrice had any inkling that either side was firmly in front. Patrice jested that knowing the Chief Justice, she would find something new that was completely wrong with both their arguments and throw out the case. Tensions in the community had been electric since the hearing ended. The Chief Operator was anxious about history repeating and the Chief Justice had warned Lidia to ensure her supporters did not congregate at the Court of Justice when she delivered her decision. It was challenging for Lidia to return to the Court during the hearing and, relieved for the excuse, she requested they stay away reminding them that regardless of the decision their journey would not end today.

The room was silent as the Chief Justice explained her reasoning. She had considered the nature of the Department

Assembly as an interim authority. Legally, she believed all that was necessary from the First Politicians was to demonstrate they had two competing parties which could fulfil the duties of the Parliament. They had done that and they had also demonstrated via the petition, which had been examined carefully, that the majority of people were satisfied with the candidates which would be available to represent their interests in Parliament. Therefore, the Chief Justice determined all the other evidence they had provided was in excess of what was legally required to satisfactorily discharge the Formation Agreement. She was, however, mindful the Formation Agreement had been designed to expire twenty years after formation and therefore found the extra caution applied by the Department Assembly at fifty years after formation was not excessive. Noting, the Department Assembly's thorough assessment of the initial request.

The Court was satisfied there were two robust competitors available and that the community in the majority wanted to return the Parliament. She did note, however, that all parties involved had neglected to address whether the core tenets of democracy were available for the symbiotic involvement required for the accountability structure of a parliamentary democracy to function. The Chief Justice, therefore, without undermining the clear will of the people to return the Parliament, ruled the end date be inserted in the Formation Agreement enabling an election in five years' time. The delay in the election date was to give the citizens of the City time to become accustomed to their new role—to hold the politicians to account. In the interim, the Department Assembly were to make all data they collected and relied upon publicly available henceforth.

The gallery erupted hugging and crying and screaming and jumping all over each other and the Court. Patrice's main concern going into the hearing had been that the change was too soon and that not enough people understood the new laws. The delay in an election was an outcome which suited everyone. Patrice and April deflated in relief.

As the room celebrated around Lidia, the noise blurred and pain washed over her. She sat forced apart from April in the building where Anna was slaughtered and all she felt was numb and drained. The grief of all she'd lost struck her down and she collapsed back into her seat. April had been watching Lidia as the decision was delivered and saw her crumple. As soon as they were dismissed, she moved across the isle and cupped her aunt's face in her hands and whispered 'I know you'd rather have her back' then helped her to stand, wrapped her arm around Lidia and walked her past the cheering crowd and out of the nightmare that stole the love of her life.

63

Once they'd left the Court, Lidia went straight to the prison to tell Diamond the verdict. The victory would not have been possible without the years they'd spent building the network which gave them the influence they needed to win. She wanted him to know without his dedication they wouldn't have made it this far. Since the day he was incarcerated, he'd written her a letter every day. With the farm, her girlfriend and her new life, it would have been easy to ignore the past and retreat into bliss. On the days when she wanted to forget and neglect her duty, his words refused to let her give up. He wouldn't let her quit.

He was excited to see her and when she told him of the decision, he was ecstatic. He would be out by the time the election was held—the only positive to waiting five years. He looked older. She apologised he was in there while they were out in the world benefiting from his sacrifice. He assured her he'd trade five years to save his City in a heartbeat.

"I know I gave you a hard time about what you did but I felt responsible. I abandoned you and pushed you away and now you're in here. I should have taken better care of you after all the years you took care of me." She cried with exhaustion. He'd never seen her cry.

"Lidia, I'm in here because I decided to fight for what I believe in. I know you thought I was too young to understand what you were doing but you forget that all those years I spent running between you all I was learning from the custodians. I saw what they did in their communities. The lives they saved by investing in people and teaching them about leadership and believing in them. They taught me to be critical, to be assertive, to stand up for myself. You were in prison far longer than I will be. People don't know what you did for this City, they think you were in India but one day they will. I will make sure they know how many years you spent keeping democracy alive so that our people could reclaim their freedom once they learned to trust again. I may be in prison but I understand what we were fighting for and you didn't put me here."

She was stunned at his eloquence and awareness and her guilt faded. She wiped away her tears and composed herself. She was exceptionally proud of the man he'd become. "I miss you. Thank you for the letters. You are the voice of my conscience some days. I'm glad to hear your girlfriend hasn't broken up with you yet."

He laughed. "She might break up with me when I tell her I want to become a campaign manager!"

She left the prison and visited Anna and told her they'd won and left some branches from her tree at the farm on her grave. Last, she went to April's father and they sat and cried for Anna and the years they'd lost to get here.

News of the election victory had spread and all those involved in the Human Chain Project – many now members of Lidia's political party – clad in their original protest outfits descended on the lanes to celebrate into the night. Exhausted from the day, Lidia rested in the Lamasery window and listened to the festivities below, waiting for her girlfriend to arrive for the party. The future she'd created was waiting for her downstairs and she couldn't wait to thank her members for their trust and dedication. Ready to start the next battle tomorrow, she looked over the City across the rooftops which had kept her company for decades and thanked them for standing tall while the people within them rediscovered their identity.

64

There was a sombre mood at the Department Ball. With the Department Assembly halved in size and the future uncertain, the ballroom was more spacious and the crowd less raucous. The ceremony began with Patrice acknowledging the awkwardness of the First Politicians taking their jobs. She pointed to the figures on the walls and remarked that they'd had the strength to form the Department Assembly when the political class was hurting the City and the time had come for them to have the strength to accept the political class had once again become the preferred leaders. She reminded them politics was just a different way of doing things and that no matter what the people decided on election day, their choice was not a reflection of the Department's exemplary service to the City. The room relaxed and their usual energy returned.

April was receiving her incoming speech from Patrice. She was irritated to be back in the spotlight but was curious to hear of all the time they'd spent together which stories Patrice cherished. The ballroom was less enthralling than April remembered. She thought perhaps the illusion of grandeur had been shattered when she'd realised how much ugliness laid behind success.

Her husband wanted them to have a baby. Looking at him next to her she knew, no matter how wretched things were outside their relationship, she was saved every time she set foot within their home. When she reflected on her life it was hard to resent the path to leadership which caused her so much anguish when it also led her to him. She too wanted a baby but secretly wished for a few more years with him to herself. Their whole lives didn't seem like enough time together.

Patrice was shuffling her notes and once the waiters cleared the last of the dinner plates, clinked her glass with a fork.

"Thank you for your attention everyone." The crowd hushed and focused. "There is one Junior Manager who doesn't need any introduction," April rolled her eyes, "because she's been a star since the second she arrived at Department East." She pointed at April and the crowd erupted shouting and clapping. "April has assured me she has had enough attention this year so I will keep this brief." Laugher rippled through the room. The joy of no privacy, April thought.

"You all know April. You know her because she works hard. You know her because she's always helping her colleagues solve problems. She's generous and kind. She's takes care of everyone. She makes sure her friends are striving to achieve excellence because she wants them to succeed." The crowd shouted in agreement at the long list of her endearing qualities. "What you don't know about April is how much she inspires me." Patrice turned and looked to April.

"One day historians will write the story of this time. That story will start with a girl in a lane who knew there was more to life than what she had been told. That girl had the courage to search in the dark for a door that might show her the path to the truth. Anyone else would have run away but you ran to the truth and demanded in the face of pain and hurt to experience life in its fullness rather than to accept a lie. April, you inspire me every day to open the door to truth and have the courage to accept whatever I find on the other side."

Their colleagues cheered for April, unaware of the toast's true meaning. April was overcome with love for her friend. Patrice spent so much time helping her to accept the responsibly she had wished wasn't hers and, for the first time, April felt worthy of the effort.

Next title from
Emma Adair

Four Chambers

Available Soon